There was nothing to alarm Mole at first.

Twigs crackled under his feet and logs tripped him, but that was all fun and exciting. It led him on, and he walked further to where the light was dimmer, and trees crouched nearer and nearer, and holes looked like ugly mouths on either side.

Everything was very still now. Twilight advanced on him steadily, gathering in all around, and the light seemed to be draining away like floodwater.

Then the faces began.

It was over his shoulder, and indistinctly, that he first thought he saw a face. It was an evil little wedge-shaped face, looking out at him from a hole. When he turned and confronted it, the thing had vanished.

A Note about *The Wind in the Willows*

The Wind in the Willows, which was written in the early 1900s, was based on a series of stories its author made up for his young son. It has been a popular book among readers young and old ever since. In fact, many adults name it as one of their all-time favorites. This kind of popularity may surprise you, considering that the characters in the book are almost all animals. But as you read *The Wind in the Willows,* you may notice that those characters—Mole, who is timid and sensible; Water Rat, an adventurer; and Toad, who is rich and incredibly full of himself—seem remarkably like human beings. While you're enjoying these charming stories, the animals' good and not-so-good points just may make you think of people you know.

The Wind *in the* Willows

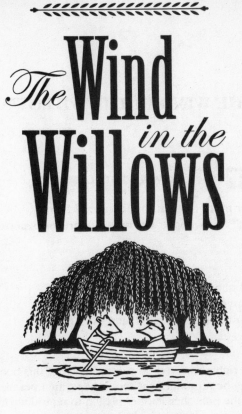

Kenneth Grahame

Edited, and with an Afterword,
by Beth Johnson

TP THE TOWNSEND LIBRARY

THE WIND IN THE WILLOWS

TP THE TOWNSEND LIBRARY

For more titles in the Townsend Library,
visit our website: **www.townsendpress.com**

Printed in the United States of America

0 9 8 7 6 5 4 3 2 1

Townsend Press, Inc.
1038 Industrial Drive
West Berlin, New Jersey 08091

ISBN 1-59194-030-3

Library of Congress Control Number:
2004104208

Table of Contents

CHAPTER 1

The River Bank

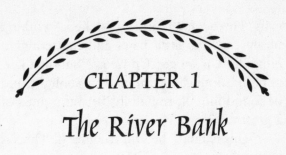

The Mole had been working very hard all morning, spring-cleaning his little home. First he swept; next he dusted. Then it was up on ladders and steps and chairs, with a brush and a pail of whitewash. Finally he had dust in his throat and eyes, and splashes of whitewash all over his black fur, and an aching back and weary arms. Spring was moving in the air above him, reaching even into his dark little underground house. Small wonder, then, that he suddenly threw his brush down on the floor, said "Bother!" and "Oh dash it!" and also "Hang spring-cleaning!" and bolted out of the house without even waiting to put on his coat. Something above was calling him in the most demanding way, and he headed for the steep little tunnel which was his house's exit. He scraped and scratched, working busily with his little paws and muttering to himself, "Up we go! Up we go!" until at last, pop! his snout came out into the sunlight, and he found himself rolling in the warm grass of a great meadow.

"This is fine!" he said to himself. "This is better than cleaning!" The sun shone hot on his fur, soft breezes caressed his face, and after living alone for so long in his underground home, the singing of happy birds sounded to him almost like a shout. The joy of living and the delight of spring made him jump into the air, and he raced across the meadow until he reached the hedge on the further side.

"Hold on there!" said an elderly rabbit at the gap in the hedge. "It's fifty cents to pass through here!" The impatient Mole knocked him over in an instant as he trotted along the side of the hedge, jeering at the other rabbits as they peeped from their holes to see what the noise was about. "Onion sauce! Onion sauce!" he said mockingly, and was gone before they could think of a good reply. Then they all started grumbling at each other. "How STUPID you are! Why didn't you tell him—" "Well, why didn't YOU say—" "You might have reminded him—" and so on, but it was much too late.

It all seemed too good to be true. He rambled busily here and there through the meadows, along the hedges, and through stands of trees. Everywhere he found birds building, flowers budding, leaves growing—everything happy and busy. And instead of having an uneasy conscience bothering him and whispering "whitewash!" he somehow only felt how wonderful it was to be the only idle dog among all these busy citizens. After all, the best part of a vacation is not to be resting yourself, but to see all the other fellows busy working.

He thought his happiness was complete when, as he wandered aimlessly along, he suddenly found himself by the edge of a full-sized river. Never in his life had he seen a river before—this sleek, full-bodied creature, chasing and chuckling, gripping things with a gurgle and leaving them with a laugh, then flinging itself on fresh playmates. The Mole was bewitched. By the side of the river he trotted, just as a small child trots with the side of a man who holds him spellbound by exciting stories. When he was tired at last, he sat on the bank, while the river still chattered on to him. It told a babbling procession of the best stories in the world.

As he sat on the grass and looked across the river, a dark hole in the opposite bank caught his eye. Dreamily, he began thinking what a nice snug house it would make for an animal who wanted a riverside residence, above flood level and far away from noise and dust. As he gazed, something bright and small seemed to twinkle down in the heart of it, vanished, then twinkled once more like a tiny star. But there could hardly be a star down in the hole, and it was too glittering and small for a glowworm. Then, as he looked, it winked at him, and he realized it was an eye. Then a small face began gradually to grow up around it, like a frame around a picture.

A brown little face, with whiskers.

A grave round face, with the same twinkle in its eye that had first attracted his notice.

Small neat ears and thick silky hair.

It was the Water Rat!

Then the two animals stood and regarded

each other cautiously.

"Hello, Mole!" said the Water Rat.

"Hello, Rat!" said the Mole.

"Would you like to come over?" asked the Rat.

"That's easy enough to SAY," said the Mole, rather irritably, as he was new to a river and riverside life and its ways.

The Rat said nothing, but stooped and unfastened a rope and pulled on it. Then he stepped into a little boat which the Mole had not noticed. It was painted blue outside and white inside, and was just the size for two animals. It captured the Mole's heart at once.

The Rat rowed quickly across the river. Then he held up his paw as the Mole stepped gingerly down. "Lean on that!" he said. "Now then, step in!" and the Mole to his surprise and delight found himself actually seated in a real boat.

"This has been a wonderful day!" said he, as the Rat shoved off and took to the oars again. "Do you know, I've never been in a boat before in all my life."

"What?" cried the Rat, open-mouthed: "Never been in a—you never—well, what have you been doing, then?"

"Is it so nice as all that?" asked the Mole shyly, though he was quite prepared to believe it. He leaned back in his seat and looked at the cushions, the oars, the rowlocks, and felt the boat sway lightly under him.

"Nice? It's the ONLY thing," said the Water Rat solemnly, as he leaned forward to row. "Believe me, my young friend, there is NOTHING—absolute nothing—half so much worth doing as simply messing about in boats. Simply messing," he went on dreamily, "messing—about—in—boats; messing—"

"Look ahead, Rat!" cried the Mole suddenly.

It was too late. The boat struck the bank hard. The dreamer lay on his back at the bottom of the boat, his heels in the air.

"—about in boats—or WITH boats," the Rat went on calmly, picking himself up with a pleasant laugh. "In or out of 'em, it doesn't matter. Nothing really seems to matter, that's the charm of it. Whether you get away, or whether you don't; whether you arrive at your destination or whether you reach somewhere else, or whether you never get anywhere at all, you're always busy. And when you've done it there's always something else to do, and you can do nothing if you like. It doesn't matter. Look here! If you really have nothing to do this morning, suppose we travel down the river together, and make a day of it?"

The Mole wiggled his toes from sheer happiness, sighed in full contentment, and leaned back blissfully into the soft cushions. "WHAT a day I'm having!" he said. "Let us start at once!"

"Hold on a minute, then!" said the Rat. He looped the rope through a ring in his landing dock, climbed up into his hole above, and soon reappeared staggering under a fat, wicker picnic basket.

"Shove that under your feet," he told the Mole, as he passed it down into the boat. Then he untied the boat and took the oars again.

"What's inside it?" asked the Mole, wriggling with curiosity.

"There's cold chicken inside it," replied the Rat briefly; "cold ham cold beef pickled gherkins salad rolls cucumber sandwiches root beer lemonade iced tea—"

"O stop, stop," cried the Mole in ecstacies: "This is too much!"

"Do you really think so?" asked the Rat seriously. "It's only what I always take on these little trips, and the other animals are always telling me that I'm a stingy beast and don't bring nearly enough!"

The Mole never heard a word he was saying. Absorbed in the new life he was entering upon, he trailed a paw in the water and dreamed long waking dreams. The Water Rat, like the good little fellow he was, rowed steadily on and didn't disturb him.

"I like your clothes awfully, old chap," he remarked after half an hour or so had passed. "I'm going to get a black velvet jacket myself some day, as soon as I can afford it."

"I beg your pardon," said the Mole, pulling himself together with an effort. "You must think I am very rude, but all this is so new to me. So this is a River!"

"THE River," corrected the Rat.

"And you really live by the river? What a jolly life!"

"By it and with it and on it and in it," said the Rat. "It's brother and sister to me, and aunts, and company, and food and drink, and (naturally) washing. It's my world, and I don't want any other. What it hasn't got isn't worth having. Lord! The times we've had together! Whether it's winter or summer, spring or autumn, it's always got its fun and its excitements."

"But isn't it a bit dull at times?" the Mole ventured to ask. "Just you and the river, and no one to talk with?"

"No one to—well, I mustn't be hard on you," said the Rat patiently. "You're new to it, and of course you don't know. The riverbank is so crowded nowadays that many people are moving away. It isn't what it used to be, at all. Otters, kingfishers, ducks, herons, all of them around all day long, always wanting you to DO something—as if a fellow had no business of his own to attend to!"

"What lies over THERE?" asked the Mole, waving a paw toward the woodland that darkly framed the water meadows on one side of the river.

"That? Oh, that's just the Wild Wood," said the Rat shortly. "We don't go there very much, we riverbankers."

"Aren't they—aren't they very NICE people in there?" said the Mole, a trifle nervously.

"W-e-ll," replied the Rat, "let me see. The squirrels are all right. AND the rabbits—some of 'em, but rabbits are a mixed lot. And then there's Badger, of course. He lives right in the heart of it; he wouldn't live anywhere else if you paid him to do it. Dear old Badger! Nobody interferes with HIM. They'd better not," he added significantly.

"Why, who WOULD interfere with him?" asked the Mole.

"Well, of course—there—are others," explained the Rat in a hesitating sort of way.

"Weasels—and stoats*—and foxes—and so on. They're all right in a way—I'm very good friends with them—but, well, you can't really trust them, and that's a fact."

The Mole knew that it is considered poor animal manners to discuss possible trouble ahead, or even to mention it, so he dropped the subject.

"And beyond the Wild Wood?" he asked "Where it's all blue and dim, and I see what may be hills, and something like the smoke of towns, or is it only clouds?"

"Beyond the Wild Wood comes the Wide World," said the Rat. "And that's something that doesn't matter, either to you or me. I've never been there, and I'm never going, nor you either, if you've got any sense at all. Don't ever refer to it again, please. Now then! Here's our backwater at last, where we're going to have lunch."

Leaving the main stream, they passed into what seemed at first like a little landlocked lake. Green grass sloped down to either edge, and brown snaky tree roots gleamed below the surface of the quiet water. Ahead of them the foamy tumble of a dam and a restless dripping mill wheel filled the air with a soothing

*A stoat, also known as an ermine, is a carnivorous forest animal common in Britain.

murmur of sound. It was so very beautiful that the Mole could only hold up both forepaws and gasp, "Oh my! Oh my! Oh my!"

The Rat brought the boat alongside the bank, tied her there, helped the still awkward Mole safely ashore, and swung out the lunch basket. The Mole begged to be allowed to unpack it all by himself, and the Rat was very pleased to indulge him. He sprawled full-length on the grass and rested, while his excited friend shook out the tablecloth and spread it, then took out all the mysterious packets one by one and arranged them, still gasping, "Oh my!" at each fresh discovery. When all was ready, the Rat said, "Now, pitch in, old fellow!" The Mole was very glad to obey, for he had started his spring-cleaning at a very early hour that morning, and had never stopped for a bite to eat.

"What are you looking at?" said the Rat presently, when the edge of their hunger was somewhat dulled, and the Mole's eyes were able to wander off the tablecloth a little.

"I am looking," said the Mole, "at a streak of bubbles that I see traveling along the surface of the water."

"Bubbles? Oho!" said the Rat, and made a cheery, inviting sort of "chirrup" noise.

A broad glistening muzzle showed itself

above the edge of the bank, and the Otter hauled himself out and shook the water from his coat.

"Greedy things!" he observed, heading toward the picnic. "Why didn't you invite me, Ratty?"

"This was just spur of the moment," explained the Rat. "By the way, this is my friend Mr. Mole."

"Pleased to meet you, I'm sure," said the Otter, and the two animals were friends immediately.

"Such a lot of activity everywhere!" continued the Otter. "All the world seems to be out on the river today. I came up this backwater to try and get a moment's peace, and then I stumbled upon you fellows! I beg your pardon—I didn't mean that quite the way it sounded, you know."

There was a rustle behind them, proceeding from a hedge still thick with last year's leaves, and a stripy head, with high shoulders behind it, peered forth at them.

"Come on, old Badger!" shouted the Rat.

The Badger trotted forward a pace or two, then grunted, "H'm! Company," and turned his back and disappeared from view.

"That's JUST the sort of fellow he is!" observed the disappointed Rat. "He simply hates Society! Now we won't see any more of him today. Well, tell us, who's out on the river?"

"Toad's out, for one," replied the Otter. "In his brand-new racing boat, with new clothes and new everything!"

The two animals looked at each other and laughed.

"Once, it was nothing but sailing," the Rat explained to Mole, "Then he tired of that and took to rafting. Nothing would please him but to raft all day and every day, and a nice mess he made of it. Last year it was houseboating, and we all had to go and stay with him in his houseboat, and pretend we liked it. He was going to spend the rest of his life in a houseboat. It's all the same, whatever he takes up; he gets tired of it, then starts on something fresh."

"He's a good fellow," remarked the Otter. "But no stability—especially in a boat!"

From where they sat they could get a glimpse of the main stream across the island that separated them, and just then a racing-boat flashed into view. The rower—a short, stout figure—was splashing badly and rolling a good deal, but working hard. The Rat stood up and called to him, but Toad—for it was he—shook his head and settled sternly to his work.

"He'll be out of the boat in a minute if he rolls like that," said the Rat, sitting down again.

"Of course he will," chuckled the Otter. "Did I ever tell you that good story about Toad and the steamboat captain? It happened this way. Toad. . . ."

A fly swerved unsteadily on top of the current in the drunken fashion of many young flies. There was a swirl of water, a "cloop!" and the fly was visible no more.

Neither was the Otter.

The Mole looked down. The voice was still in his ears, but the grass on which he had sprawled was empty. Not an Otter could be seen.

But again there was a streak of bubbles on the surface of the river.

The Rat hummed a tune, and the Mole remembered that polite animals never comment on the sudden disappearance of one's friends at any moment, for any reason or no reason whatever.

"Well, well," said the Rat, "I suppose we ought to be moving. I wonder which of us had better pack the lunch basket?" He did not speak as if he was frightfully eager for the treat.

"Oh, please let me," said the Mole. So, of course, the Rat let him.

Packing the basket is never as pleasant work as unpacking the basket. But the Mole was determined to enjoy everything, and although just when he had got the basket packed and strapped up tightly he saw a plate staring up at him from the grass...and when the job had been done again the Rat pointed out a fork...and last of all, behold! the mustard pot, which he had been sitting on without noticing...still, somehow, the thing got finished at last, without much loss of temper.

The afternoon sun was getting low as the Rat rowed gently homeward in a dreamy mood, murmuring poetry to himself, and not paying much attention to Mole. But the Mole was very full of lunch, and self-satisfaction, and already feeling quite at home in a boat, or so he thought. He was getting a bit restless, and he said, "Ratty! Please, I want to row now!"

The Rat shook his head with a smile. "Not yet, my young friend," he said—"wait until you've had a few lessons. It's not so easy as it looks."

The Mole was quiet for a minute or two. But he began to feel more and more jealous of Rat, rowing so easily along, and his pride began to whisper that he could do it every bit as well. He jumped up and grabbed the oars, so suddenly that the Rat was taken by surprise and fell backward off his seat with his legs in the air for the second time. The triumphant Mole took his place and grabbed the oars with great confidence.

"Stop it, you silly ass!" cried the Rat, from the bottom of the boat. "You'll tip us over!"

The Mole flung the oars back with a flourish, and made a great dig at the water. He missed the surface altogether, his legs flew up above his head, and he found himself lying on the top of the Rat. Greatly alarmed, he made a grab at the side of the boat, and the next moment—Sploosh!

Over went the boat, and he found himself struggling in the river.

Oh, how cold the water was, and how VERY wet it felt. How it sang in his ears as he went down, down, down! How bright and welcome the sun looked as he rose to the surface coughing and spluttering! How awful was his despair when he felt himself sinking again! Then a firm paw gripped him by the back of his neck. It was the Rat, and he was evidently laughing—the Mole could FEEL him laughing, right down his arm and through his paw.

The Rat got hold of an oar and shoved it under the Mole's arm. Then he did the same to the other side of him and, swimming behind, propelled the helpless animal to shore, hauled him out, and set him down on the bank, a squashy, pulpy lump of misery.

When the Rat had rubbed him down a bit, and wrung some of the wet out of him, he said, "Now, then, old fellow! Trot up and down in the sun until you're warm and dry again, while I dive for the lunch basket."

So the dismal Mole, wet and ashamed, trotted about till he was nearly dry. Meanwhile the Rat plunged into the water again, recovered the boat, fetched his floating property to shore bit by bit, and finally dived successfully for the lunch basket and struggled to land with it.

When they were ready to start once more, the Mole, limp and depressed, took his seat in the boat. As they set off, he said in a low voice, "Ratty, my generous friend! I am very sorry for my foolish conduct. My heart nearly stops when I think how I might have lost that beautiful lunch basket. I have been a complete ass, and I know it. Will you overlook it this once and forgive me, and let us start over again?"

"That's all right, bless you!" responded the Rat cheerily. "What's a little wet to a Water Rat? Don't you think any more about it. And, look here! I really think you had better come and stay with me for a little while. It's very plain and rough, you know—not like Toad's house at all—but you haven't seen that yet. Still, I can make you comfortable. And I'll teach you to row, and to swim, and you'll soon be as handy on the water as any of us."

The Mole was so touched by this kind offer that he could barely answer, and he had to brush away a tear or two with the back of his paw. But the Rat kindly looked in another direction, and soon the Mole's spirits revived. He was even able to give a clever retort to a couple of ducks who were snickering about his bedraggled appearance.

When they got home, the Rat fetched the Mole a warm robe and slippers, made a bright fire in the parlor, planted him in an armchair before the fire, and told him river stories till suppertime. Very thrilling stories they were, too, to an earth-dwelling animal like Mole. There were stories about dams, and sudden floods, and leaping pike, and steamships, and about herons, and night fishing with Otter, or long excursions with Badger. Supper was a most cheerful meal, and very soon afterward the sleepy Mole was shown upstairs to the best bedroom, where he soon laid his head on his pillow in great peace and contentment.

This day was only the first of many like it for the newly liberated Mole. He learned to swim and to row, and entered fully into the joy of river life.

CHAPTER 2

The Open Road

"Ratty," said the Mole suddenly, one bright summer morning, "if you please, I want to ask you a favor."

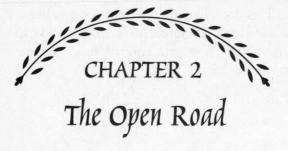

The Rat was sitting on the riverbank, singing a little song. He had just composed it himself, so he was concentrating very hard, and not paying attention to Mole or anything else. Since early morning he had been swimming in the river with his friends the ducks. And when the ducks stood on their heads suddenly, as ducks will, he would dive down and tickle their necks until they were forced to come to the surface again in a hurry. They were spluttering and angry and shaking their feathers at him, for it is impossible to say what you feel when your head is under water. At last they begged him to go away and mind his own business. So the Rat went away, and sat on the riverbank in the sun, and made up a song about them, which he called:

DUCKS' DITTY

All along the backwater,
Through the rushes tall,
Ducks are a-dabbling,
Up tails all!

Ducks' tails, drakes' tails,
Yellow feet a-quiver,
Yellow bills all out of sight
Busy in the river!

Slushy green undergrowth
Where the perch swim—
Here we keep our parlor,
Cool and full and dim.

Everyone for what he likes!
WE like to be
Heads down, tails up,
Dabbling fr e!

High in the blue above
Swallows whirl and call—
WE are down a-dabbling
Up tails all!

"I don't like that little song VERY much, Rat," said the Mole cautiously. He was no poet himself and didn't care who knew it, and he had an honest nature.

"Neither did the ducks," replied the Rat cheerfully. "They say, 'WHY can't fellows do what they like WHEN they like, without other fellows sitting on banks and watching them and making remarks and poetry and things about them? What NONSENSE it all is!' That's what the ducks say."

"They're right, they're right," said the Mole, heartily.

"No, they aren't!" cried the Rat indignantly.

"Well then, they aren't," replied the Mole soothingly. "But what I wanted to ask you was, won't you take me to visit Mr. Toad? I've heard so much about him, and I want to meet him."

"Why, certainly," said the good-natured Rat, jumping to his feet and dismissing poetry from his mind. "Get the boat out, and we'll paddle up there at once. It's never the wrong time to call on Toad. Early or late, he's always glad to see you, always sorry when you go!"

"He must be a very nice animal," observed the Mole, as he got into the boat and took the oars.

"He is indeed the best of animals," replied Rat. "So good-natured, and so affectionate. Perhaps he's not very clever—we can't all be geniuses—and he may be both boastful and conceited. But he has got some great qualities, has Toady."

Rounding a bend in the river, they came in sight of a handsome, dignified old house of mellowed red brick, with well-kept lawns reaching down to the water's edge.

"There's Toad Hall," said the Rat, "and that creek on the left leads to his boathouse, where we'll leave the boat. The stables are over there to the right. That's the banquet hall you're looking at now—very old, that is. Toad is rather rich, you know, and this is really one of the nicest houses around here, though we never admit that to Toad."

They glided up the creek, into the shadow of a large boathouse. Here they saw many handsome boats, slung from the cross beams or hauled up on piers, but none in the water. The place had an unused and a deserted air.

The Rat looked around him. "I understand," said he. "Boating is played out. He's tired of it. I wonder what new fad he has taken up now? Come along and let's find him. We shall hear all about it soon enough."

They climbed out of the boat and strolled across the bright flower-decked lawns in search of Toad, whom they found resting in a wicker garden-chair. He had a preoccupied expression on his face and a large map spread out on his knees.

"Hooray!" he cried as he saw them, jumping up, "this is splendid!" He shook the paws of both of them warmly, never waiting for an introduction to the Mole. "How KIND of you!" he went on, dancing around them in delight. "I was just going to send a boat down the river for you, Ratty, with strict orders that you were to be fetched up here at once. I need you badly—both of you. Now what would you like to eat or drink? Come inside and have something! You don't know how lucky it is, your turning up just now!"

"Let's just sit for a bit, Toady!" said the Rat, throwing himself into another lawn chair, while the Mole made some polite remark about Toad's "delightful residence."

"Finest house on the whole river," cried Toad loudly. "Or anywhere else, for that matter," he could not help adding.

Here the Rat nudged the Mole. Unfortunately the Toad saw him do it, and turned very red. There was a moment's painful silence. Then Toad burst out laughing. "All right, Ratty," he said. "It's just the way I am, you know. And it's not such a bad house, is it? You know you like it yourself. Now, look here. You are the very animals I want. You've got to help me. It's most important!"

"It's about your rowing, I suppose," said the Rat innocently. "You're getting on fairly well, although you still splash a good bit. With a great deal of patience and coaching, you may—"

"O, pooh! Boating!" interrupted the Toad, in great disgust. 'Silly childish amusement. I've given that up LONG ago. Sheer waste of time, that's what it is. It makes me downright sorry to see you fellows spending all your energies in that aimless manner. No, I've discovered the real thing, the only genuine occupation for a lifetime. I plan to devote the remainder of my life to it, and I'm only sorry that I wasted so many years in silly activities. Come with me, dear Ratty, and your amiable friend also, just as far as the stable yard. You shall see!"

He led the way to the stable yard, the Rat following with a most mistrustful expression. There they saw a shining new gypsy caravan, painted canary-yellow trimmed with green. Its wheels were red.

"There you are!" cried the Toad, puffing himself up with pride. "There's real life for you, embodied in that little cart. The open road, the dusty highway, the meadows, the town squares, the hedges, the rolling hills! Camps, villages, towns, cities! Here today, off to somewhere else tomorrow! Travel, change, interest, excitement! The whole world before you, and a horizon that's always changing! And notice, this is the very finest cart of its sort, without any exception. Come inside and look at the arrangements. Planned 'em all myself, I did!"

The Mole was tremendously interested and excited, and followed him eagerly up the steps and into the caravan. The Rat stayed where he was, only snorting and thrusting his hands deep into his pockets.

It was indeed very compact and comfortable. There were little sleeping bunks; a little table that folded up against the wall; a stove, lockers, bookshelves; a bird-cage with a bird in it; and pots, pans, jugs and kettles of every size and variety.

"All complete!" said the Toad triumphantly, pulling open a cupboard. "You see—cookies, canned lobster, sardines—everything you can possibly want. Soda water here—tobacco there—writing paper, bacon, jam, cards and dominoes." He continued, as they descended the steps again, "You'll find that nothing whatever has been forgotten, when we start this afternoon."

"I beg your pardon," said the Rat slowly, as he chewed a straw, "but did I overhear you say something about 'WE,' and 'START,' and 'THIS AFTERNOON?'"

"Now, dear good old Ratty," said Toad, imploringly, "don't go all stiff and sniffy on me, because you know you've GOT to come. I can't possibly manage without you, so please consider it settled, and don't argue. You surely don't mean to stick to your dull old river all your life, and just live in a hole, and go BOATING? I want to show you the world! I'm going to make an ANIMAL of you, my boy!"

"I don't care," said the Rat, doggedly. "I'm not coming, and that's flat. And I AM going to stick to my old river, AND live in a hole, AND boat, as I've always done. And what's more, Mole's going to stick with me and do as I do, aren't you, Mole?"

"Of course I am," said the Mole, loyally. "I'll always stick to you, Rat. All the same, it sounds as if it might have been—well, rather fun, you know!" he added, wistfully. Poor Mole! This adventurous life was so new to him, and so thrilling, and this fresh idea was so tempting. And besides, he had fallen in love at first sight with the canary-colored cart and all its contents.

The Rat saw what was in his mind, and wavered. He hated disappointing people, and he was fond of the Mole, and would do almost anything to make him happy. Toad was watching both of them closely.

"Come along in, and have some lunch," he said, diplomatically, "and we'll talk it over. We don't need to decide anything in a hurry. Of course, I don't really care. I only want to give pleasure to you fellows. 'Live for others!' That's my motto in life."

During lunch—which was excellent, as everything at Toad Hall always was—the Toad really let himself go. Ignoring the Rat, he played upon the inexperienced Mole as a master musician plays a violin. He described the trip and the joys of the open life in such glowing colors that the Mole could hardly sit still. Somehow, it was soon taken for granted that the trip was a settled thing, and the Rat let his good nature overcome his objections. He could not bear to disappoint his two friends, who were already happily planning each day's activities for several weeks ahead.

When they were quite ready, the triumphant Toad led his companions to the pasture and told them to capture the old gray horse. The horse was greatly annoyed, and he took a good deal of catching. Meanwhile, Toad packed the cupboards even tighter with necessities, and hung nosebags, nets of

onions, bundles of hay, and baskets from the bottom of the cart. At last the horse was caught and harnessed and they set off, all talking at once. Each animal either trudged by the side of the cart or sat on the seat, whichever he preferred. It was a golden afternoon. The smell of the dust they kicked up was rich and satisfying; out of the orchards on either side of the road, birds called and whistled to them cheerily. Good-natured wayfarers told them "Good day," or stopped to say nice things about their beautiful cart; and rabbits, sitting at their front doors in the hedges, held up their forepaws and said, "Oh my! Oh my! Oh my!"

Late in the evening, tired and happy and

miles from home, they stopped in a field far from any houses, turned the horse loose to graze, and ate their simple supper sitting on the grass. Toad talked big about all he was going to do in the days to come, while the stars grew full and bright all around them, and the yellow moon came to keep them company. At last they turned in to their little bunks in the cart. Toad sleepily said, "Well, good night, you fellows! This is the real life for a gentleman! Talk about your old river!"

"I DON'T talk about my river," replied the patient Rat. "You KNOW I don't, Toad. But I THINK about it," he added sadly, in a lower tone. "I think about it—all the time!"

The Mole reached out from under his blanket, found the Rat's paw in the darkness, and gave it a squeeze. "I'll do whatever you like, Ratty," he whispered. "Shall we run away tomorrow morning, quite early, and go back to our dear old hole on the river?"

"No, we'll see it out," whispered back the Rat. "Thanks awfully, but I ought to stick by Toad until this trip is ended. It wouldn't be safe for him to be left to himself. It won't last very long. His fads never do. Good night!"

The end was nearer than even the Rat suspected.

After so much open air and excitement

the Toad slept very soundly, and no amount of shaking could wake him the next morning. So the Mole and Rat went to work, and while the Rat cared for the horse, and lit a fire, and cleaned last night's cups and platters, and got things ready for breakfast, the Mole trudged off to the nearest village for milk and eggs and various necessities the Toad had, of course, forgotten. The hard work had all been done, and the two animals were thoroughly exhausted, by the time Toad appeared. He was fresh and cheery, and kept remarking what a pleasant easy life it was they were all leading now, compared with the cares and worries of housekeeping at home.

They had a pleasant ramble that day over grassy hills and along narrow lanes, and camped as before on a field, only this time the two guests took care that Toad did his fair share of work. As a result, when the time came for starting next morning, Toad was by now not nearly so happy about the simple life. In fact, he attempted to return to bed, from which he was hauled by force. They traveled, as before, across the country by narrow lanes. It was not until the afternoon that they came out on their first highway. And there disaster, swift and unexpected, sprang out on them. The disaster was important enough to their trip, but it proved simply overwhelming in its effect on the life of Toad.

They were strolling along the highway. The Mole was by the horse's head, talking to him, since the horse had complained that he was being frightfully left out of it. The Toad and the Water Rat were walking behind the cart talking together—at least Toad was talking, and Rat was saying occasionally, "Yes, precisely; and what did YOU say to HIM?"—and thinking all the time of something very different, when far behind them they heard a faint sound. It sounded like, "Poop-poop."

Hardly noticing it, they resumed their conversation, when in what seemed only an instant the peaceful scene changed. With a blast of wind and a whirl of sound that made them jump for the nearest ditch, IT was on them! "Poop-poop" rang again in their ears, and they had a moment's glimpse of glittering glass and rich leather. The magnificent motor-car (for that is what it was) possessed all earth and air for the fraction of a second. It flung up a cloud of dust that blinded and enwrapped them completely, and then dwindled to a speck in the far distance.

The old gray horse had been dreaming, as he plodded along, of his quiet pasture. Faced with a wholly new situation such as this, he simply abandoned himself to his natural emotions. Rearing, plunging, backing up, in spite of all the Mole's efforts, he drove the cart backward toward the deep ditch at the side of the road. It wavered an instant—there was a heartrending crash—and the canary-colored cart lay on its side in the ditch, a hopeless wreck.

The Rat danced up and down in the road, simply out of his head with rage. "You villains!" he shouted, shaking both fists, "You scoundrels, you highwaymen, you—you—roadhogs! I'll have the law on you! I'll report you! I'll take you through all the courts!" His homesickness had quite slipped away, and for the moment he was the captain of a canary-colored ship driven onto the rocks by the reckless actions of pirates.

Toad sat straight down in the middle of the dusty road, his legs stretched out before him, and stared in the direction of the disappearing motorcar. His face wore a peaceful, satisfied expression, and at intervals he faintly murmured "Poop-poop!"

The Mole was busy trying to quiet the horse, which he succeeded in doing after a time. Then he went to look at the cart, on its side in the ditch. It was indeed a sorry sight. Panels and windows smashed, axles hopelessly bent, one wheel off, sardine tins scattered over the wide world, and the bird in the bird-cage sobbing pitifully and calling to be let out.

The Rat came to help him, but their efforts were not enough to raise the cart. “Hey! Toad!” they cried. “Come and lend a hand, can’t you?”

The Toad never answered a word, or budged from his seat in the road, so they went to see what was the matter with him. They found him in a sort of a trance, a happy smile on his face, his eyes still fixed on the dusty wake of their destroyer. At intervals he still murmured, “Poop-poop!”

The Rat shook him by the shoulder. “Are you coming to help us, Toad?” he demanded sternly.

“Glorious, stirring sight!” murmured Toad, never offering to move. “The poetry of motion! The REAL way to travel! The ONLY way to travel! Villages skipped, towns and cities jumped—always somebody else’s horizon! Oh bliss! Oh poop-poop! Oh my! Oh my!”

“Oh, STOP being an ass, Toad!” cried the Mole in despair.

“And to think I never KNEW!” went on the Toad in a dreamy monotone. “All those wasted years that lie behind me, I never knew, never even DREAMED! But NOW—now that I know, now that I fully realize! What dust-clouds shall spring up behind me as I speed on my reckless way! What carts I shall fling carelessly into the ditch in the wake of my magnificent progress! Horrid little carts—common carts—canary-colored carts!"

"What are we to do with him?" asked the Mole of the Water Rat.

"Nothing at all," replied the Rat firmly. "There is really nothing to be done. You see, I've known him a long time. He is possessed. He has got a new craze, and it always affects him like this, in its first stage. He'll be like this for days now, like an animal walking in a happy dream, quite useless. Never mind him. Let's go and see what there is to be done about the cart."

A careful inspection showed them that, even if they succeeded in putting it upright, the cart could travel no longer. The axles were in a hopeless state, and the missing wheel was shattered into pieces.

The Rat knotted the horse's reins over his back and led him by a rope, carrying the bird-cage and its hysterical occupant in the other hand. "Come on!" he said grimly to the Mole. "It's five or six miles to the nearest town, and we shall just have to walk. The sooner we start the better."

"But what about Toad?" asked the Mole anxiously, as they set off together. "We can't leave him there, sitting in the middle of the road! It's not safe. Suppose another Thing comes along?"

"Oh, BOTHER Toad," said the Rat savagely. "I'm done with him!"

They had not proceeded very far on their way, however, when there was a pattering of feet behind them, and Toad caught up and took an arm of each, still breathing quickly and staring into space.

"Now, look here, Toad!" said the Rat sharply, "as soon as we get to the town, you'll have to go straight to the police station, and see if they know anything about that motor-car and who it belongs to, and file a complaint. And then you'll have to go to a blacksmith's or a wheelwright's and arrange for the cart to be fetched and mended. It'll take time, but it's not quite a hopeless smash. Meanwhile, the Mole and I will go to an inn and find rooms where we can stay until the cart's ready, and until your nerves have recovered from the shock."

"Police station! Complaint!" murmured Toad dreamily. "Me COMPLAIN of that beautiful, that heavenly vision that has been granted me! Mend the cart! I'm done with carts forever. I never want to see the cart, or to hear of it, again. Oh, Ratty! You can't think how grateful I am to you for coming on this trip! I wouldn't have gone without you, and then I might never have seen that—that swan, that sunbeam, that thunderbolt! I might never have heard that entrancing sound, or smelled that bewitching smell! I owe it all to you, my best of friends!"

The Rat turned away from him in despair. "You see how it is?" he said to the Mole, speaking across Toad's head. "He's quite hopeless. I give up—when we get to the town we'll go to the railway station, and with luck we may catch a train that'll get us back to the riverbank tonight. And if ever you catch me going anywhere with this maddening animal again . . ."

He snorted, and during the rest of that weary trudge spoke only to Mole.

On reaching the town they went straight to the station and deposited Toad in the waiting room, giving a porter a dollar to keep an eye on him. They then left the horse at a stable, and gave what instructions they could about the cart and its contents. Eventually, having taken a slow train to a station not very far from Toad Hall, they escorted the spellbound, sleepwalking Toad to his door, put him inside it, and told his housekeeper to put him to bed. Then they got out their boat from the boathouse, rowed down the river, and at a very late hour sat down to supper in their own cozy riverside parlor, to the Rat's great contentment.

The following evening the Mole, who had risen late and taken things very easy all day, was sitting on the bank fishing. Along came the Rat, who had been looking up his friends and gossiping. "Heard the news?" he said. "There's nothing else being talked about, all along the riverbank. Toad went up to Town by an early train this morning. And he has ordered a large and very expensive motorcar."

CHAPTER 3

The Wild Wood

The Mole had long wanted to meet the Badger. He seemed, by all accounts, to be an important character. Although he was rarely visible, his unseen influence was felt by everybody about the place. But whenever the Mole mentioned his wish to the Water Rat, he found himself put off. "It's all right," the Rat would say. "Badger'll turn up some day or other, and then I'll introduce you. He's the best of fellows! But you see him only when he wants to be seen."

"Couldn't you ask him here for dinner or something?" said the Mole.

"He wouldn't come," replied the Rat simply. "Badger hates Society, and invitations, and dinner, and all that sort of thing."

"Well, then, suppose we go and visit HIM?" suggested the Mole.

"Oh, he wouldn't like that at ALL," said the Rat, quite alarmed. "He's so very shy, I'm sure he'd be offended. I've never dared to call on him at his own home myself, though I know him so well. Besides, we can't. It's quite out of the question, because he lives in the very middle of the Wild Wood."

"Well, what if he does?" said the Mole. "You told me the Wild Wood was all right."

"Oh, I know, I know, it is," replied the Rat evasively. "But I don't think we should go there just now. Not JUST yet. It's a long way, and he wouldn't be at home at this time of year anyhow, and he'll show up some day, if you'll wait quietly."

The Mole had to be content with this. But the Badger never came along. Every day was busy and amusing, and it was not until summer was long over, and cold and frost kept them indoors, that he found himself thinking again about the solitary gray Badger, who lived by himself in his hole in the middle of the Wild Wood.

In the wintertime the Rat slept a great deal, going to bed early and rising late. During his short day he sometimes scribbled poetry or did small domestic jobs about the house. There were always animals dropping in for a chat, so there was a good deal of storytelling and comparing notes about the past summer and all that they had done. Still, the Mole had a good deal of spare time on his hands. So it was that one afternoon, when the Rat was in his armchair, sometimes dozing and sometimes trying out rhymes, he decided to go by himself to explore the Wild Wood, and perhaps meet Mr. Badger.

It was a cold still afternoon with a hard steely sky overhead, when he slipped out of the warm parlor into the open air. The country lay naked and leafless around him. He liked the bareness of the winter landscape, and with great cheerfulness he headed toward the Wild Wood, which lay before him low and threatening, like a black reef in some quiet southern sea.

There was nothing to alarm Mole at first. Twigs crackled under his feet and logs tripped him, but that was all fun and exciting. It led him on, and he walked further to where the light was dimmer, and trees crouched nearer and nearer, and holes looked like ugly mouths on either side.

Everything was very still now. Twilight advanced on him steadily, gathering in all around, and the light seemed to be draining away like floodwater.

Then the faces began.

It was over his shoulder, and indistinctly, that he first thought he saw a face. It was an evil little wedge-shaped face, looking out at him from a hole. When he turned and confronted it, the thing had vanished.

He walked more quickly, telling himself cheerfully not to begin imagining things. He passed another hole, and another, and another, and then—yes!— no!—yes! Certainly a little narrow face, with hard eyes, had flashed up for an instant from a hole, and was gone. He hesitated—braced himself up for an effort and walked on. Then suddenly, every hole, far and near (and there were hundreds of them), seemed to possess a face. All of them were staring with looks of malice and hatred, hard-eyed and evil and sharp.

If he could only get away from the holes, he thought, there would be no more faces. He swung off the path and plunged into the deeper woods.

Then the whistling began.

It was very faint and shrill when he first heard it, and far behind him; but somehow it made him hurry forward. Then, still very faint and shrill, it sounded far ahead of him, and made him hesitate and want to go back. As he halted in confusion, it broke out on either side of him. Then it seemed to be caught up and passed on throughout the whole length of the woods. They were ready for him, whoever they were! And he—he was alone, and unarmed, and far from any help, and it was getting dark.

Then the pattering noise began.

The noise was so slight and delicate, he thought at first it was only falling leaves. Then as it grew it took on a regular rhythm, and he knew it could only be the pat-pat-pat of little feet a very long way off. Was it in front or behind him? It seemed to be first one, and then the other, then both. It grew and it multiplied as he listened anxiously, until it seemed to be closing in on him. As he stood still listening, a rabbit came running through the trees, headed straight for him. He waited, expecting it to slow down, or to swerve away to avoid him. Instead, the animal almost brushed him as it dashed past, his face set and hard, his eyes staring. "Get out of here, you fool, get out!" the Mole heard him mutter as he swung round a stump and disappeared down a friendly burrow.

The pattering increased until it sounded like sudden hail on the dry carpet of leaves spread around him. The whole woods seemed running now, running hard, hunting, chasing, closing in around something or—somebody? In panic, he too began to run, blindly. He ran up against things, he fell over things and into things, he darted under things and dodged around things. At last he took refuge in the deep dark hollow of an old beech tree, which offered shelter—perhaps even safety, but who could tell? Anyhow, he was too tired to run any further, and could only snuggle down into the dry leaves and hope he was safe for a time. And as he lay there panting and trembling, and listened to the whistlings and the patterings outside, he knew it at last. It was that dread thing which the Rat had tried to shield him from—the Terror of the Wild Wood!

Meantime the Rat, warm and comfortable, dozed by his fireside. His paper of half-finished poems slipped from his knee, his head fell back, and he wandered in his dreams along the grassy banks of the river. Then a coal slipped, the fire crackled and sent up a spurt of flame, and he woke with a start. Remembering what he had been doing, he reached down to the floor for his verses, then looked around for the Mole to ask him if he knew a good rhyme for something or other.

But the Mole was not there.

He listened for a time. The house seemed very quiet.

Then he called "Moly!" several times, and, receiving no answer, got up and went out into the hall.

The Mole's cap was missing from its accustomed peg. His boots, which always lay by the umbrella stand, were also gone.

The Rat left the house and carefully examined the muddy surface of the ground outside, hoping to find the Mole's tracks. There they were, sure enough. The boots were new, just bought for the winter, and the treads on their soles were fresh and sharp. He could see the imprints of them in the mud, running along straight and purposeful, directly to the Wild Wood.

The Rat looked very grave, and stood in deep thought for a minute or two. Then he reentered the house, strapped a belt round his waist, shoved a pair of pistols into it, took up a heavy club, and set off quickly for the Wild Wood.

It was already getting toward dusk when he reached the first fringe of trees and plunged into the woods, looking anxiously for any sign of his friend. Here and there wicked little faces popped out of holes, but vanished immediately at sight of the brave animal, his pistols, and the great ugly club in his hand. The whistling and pattering which he had heard quite plainly when he entered died away, and all was very still. He made his way through the length of the wood, to its furthest edge. Then, leaving the path, he began criss-crossing the entire area, and all the time calling out cheerfully, "Moly, Moly, Moly! Where are you? It's me—it's old Rat!"

He had patiently hunted through the woods for an hour or more, when at last, to his joy, he heard a little answering cry. Guiding himself by the sound, he made his way through the twilight to the foot of an old beech tree with a hole in it. From out of the hole came a feeble voice, saying "Ratty! Is that really you?"

The Rat crept into the hollow, and there he found the Mole, exhausted and still trembling. "Oh Rat!" he cried, "I've been so frightened, you can't think!"

"Oh, I quite understand," said the Rat soothingly. "You really shouldn't have gone, Mole. I did my best to stop you. We river-bankers, we hardly ever come here by ourselves. If we have to come, we come in pairs, at least; then we're generally all right. Besides, there are a hundred things one has to know, which we understand and you don't yet. I mean passwords, and signs, and sayings which have power, and plants you carry in your pocket, and verses you repeat, and dodges and tricks you practice. They're all simple enough when you know them, but you've got to know them if you're a small animal, or you'll get in trouble. Of course if you were Badger or Otter, it would be quite another matter."

"Surely brave Mr. Toad wouldn't mind coming here by himself, would he?" asked the Mole.

"Old Toad?" said the Rat, laughing heartily. "He wouldn't show his face here alone, not for a whole hatful of gold, Toad wouldn't."

The Mole was greatly cheered by the sound of the Rat's careless laughter, as well as by the sight of his stick and his gleaming pistols. He stopped shivering and began to feel bolder and more like himself again.

"Now then," said the Rat presently, "we really must pull ourselves together and start for home while there's still a little light. We can't spend the night here, you understand. Too cold, for one thing."

"Dear Ratty," said the poor Mole, "I'm dreadfully sorry, but I'm dead beat and that's a fact. You MUST let me rest here a while longer, and get my strength back, if I'm to get home at all."

"Oh, all right," said the good-natured Rat, "rest away. It's pretty nearly pitch dark now, anyhow, and there ought to be a bit of a moon later."

So the Mole curled into the dry leaves and presently dropped off into an uneasy sleep. The Rat covered himself up too, as best he could, and lay waiting, with a pistol in his paw.

The Mole woke up at last, feeling much better. The Rat said, "Now then! I'll just take a look outside and see if everything's quiet, and then we really must be off."

He went to the entrance of their retreat and put his head out. Then the Mole heard him saying quietly to himself, "Oh my! Now this is something!"

"What's up, Ratty?" asked the Mole.

"SNOW is up," replied the Rat briefly; "or rather, DOWN. It's snowing hard."

The Mole came and crouched beside him, and, looking out, saw that the woods that had been so dreadful to him looked quite different. Holes, hollows, pools, pitfalls, and other black menaces were vanishing fast, and a gleaming carpet of snow was springing up everywhere.

"Well, well, it can't be helped," said the Rat. "We must make a start, and take our chances. The problem is, I don't exactly know where we are. And now this snow makes everything look so very different."

It did indeed. The Mole would not have known that it was the same woods. However, they set out bravely in the direction that seemed most promising, holding on to each other and pretending to feel very brave and cheerful.

An hour or two later—they had lost all count of time—they stopped, weary and hopelessly lost, and sat down on a fallen tree-trunk to consider what to do. They were aching with fatigue and bruised with tumbles; they had fallen into several holes and got thoroughly wet; the snow was getting so deep that they could hardly drag their little legs through it, and the trees were thicker and looked more alike than ever. There seemed to be no end to this woods, and no beginning, and, worst of all, no way out.

"We can't sit here very long," said the Rat. "We shall have to keep going, and do something or other. The cold is too awful, and the snow will soon be too deep for us to wade through." He peered about him and considered. "This is what occurs to me," he went on. "There's a sort of valley down here in front of us, where the ground seems all hilly and humpy. We'll make our way down into that, and try and find some sort of shelter, a cave or hole with a dry floor, out of the snow and the wind. There we'll have a good rest before we try again. Besides, the snow may stop, or something may turn up."

So once more they got on their feet, and struggled down into the valley, where they hunted for a cave or some corner that was dry and protected from the harsh wind and the whirling snow. They were investigating one of the hilly bits the Rat had spoken of, when suddenly the Mole tripped and fell forward on his face with a squeal.

"Oh my leg!" he cried. "Oh my poor shin!" and he sat up on the snow holding his leg in both his front paws.

"Poor old Mole!" said the Rat kindly. "You don't seem to be having much luck today, do you? Let's have a look at the leg.

You've cut your shin, sure enough. Wait till I get at my handkerchief, and I'll tie it up for you."

"I must have tripped over a hidden branch," said the Mole miserably. "Oh, my! Oh, my!"

"It's a very clean cut," said the Rat, examining it again. "That was never done by a branch or a stump. Looks as if it was made by a sharp metal edge of something. Funny!" He thought a while, and examined the humps and slopes that surrounded them.

"Well, never mind what done it," said the Mole, forgetting his grammar in his pain. "It hurts just the same, whatever done it."

But the Rat, after carefully tying up the leg with his handkerchief, had left him and was busy scraping in the snow. He scratched and shoveled and explored, all four legs working busily, while the Mole waited impatiently, remarking, "Oh, come ON, Rat!"

Suddenly the Rat cried "Hooray!" and then "Hooray-oo-ray-oo-ray-oo-ray!" and actually began dancing in the snow.

"What HAVE you found, Ratty?" asked the Mole, still nursing his leg.

"Come and see!" said the delighted Rat, as he jigged on.

The Mole hobbled up to the spot and had

a good look.

"Well," he said at last, slowly, "I SEE it, all right. I've seen the same sort of thing before, lots of times. Familiar object, I call it. A foot-scraper! Well, what of it? Why dance around a foot-scraper?"

"But don't you see what it MEANS, you—you dull-witted animal?" cried the Rat impatiently.

"Of course I see what it means," replied the Mole. "It simply means that some VERY careless and forgetful person has left his foot-scraper lying about in the middle of the Wild Wood, just where it's sure to trip somebody up. Very thoughtless of him, I call it. When I get home I shall go and complain about it to—to somebody or other, see if I don't!"

"Oh dear!" cried the Rat, in despair at the Mole's thickheadedness. "Here, stop arguing and come and scrape!" And he set to work again and made the snow fly in all directions around him.

After some further work his efforts were rewarded, and a very shabby doormat was exposed to view.

"There, what did I tell you?" exclaimed the Rat in great triumph.

"Absolutely nothing," replied the Mole, quite truthfully. "Well now," he went on, "you seem to have found another piece of domestic litter, and I suppose you're perfectly happy. Better go ahead and dance around that if you've got to, and get it over, and then perhaps we can go on and not waste any more time over garbage heaps. Can we EAT a doormat? Or sleep under a doormat? Or sit on a doormat and ride home over the snow on it, you exasperating rodent?"

"Do—you—mean—to—say," cried the excited Rat, "that this doormat doesn't TELL you anything?"

"Really, Rat," said the Mole, quite irritably, "I think we've had enough of this foolishness. Who ever heard of a doormat TELLING anyone anything? They simply don't do it. They are not like that at all. Doormats know their place."

"Now look here, you—you stupid beast," replied the Rat, really angry, "this must stop. Not another word, but scrape—scrape and scratch and dig and hunt around, especially on the sides of the hills, if you want to sleep dry and warm tonight, for it's our last chance!"

The Rat attacked the snowbank beside them with great energy, probing with his stick everywhere and then digging with fury. The Mole scraped busily too, more to please the

Rat than for any other reason, for he really thought that his friend was losing his mind.

After ten minutes of hard work, the point of the Rat's stick struck something that sounded hollow. He worked till he could get a paw through, and then he called the Mole to come and help him. The two animals worked hard, until at last the result of their labors stood visible before the astonished Mole.

In the side of what had seemed to be a plain snowbank stood a solid-looking little door, painted dark green. An iron bell-pull hung by the side, and below it, on a small brass plate, neatly engraved in square capital letters, they could read by the aid of moonlight:

MR. BADGER.

The Mole fell backward in the snow from sheer surprise and delight. "Rat!" he cried apologetically, "you're a wonder! A real wonder, that's what you are. I see it all now! You thought it out, step by step, in that wise head of yours, from the very moment that I fell and cut my shin. You looked at the cut, and at once your majestic mind said to itself, 'Footscraper!' And then you went to work and found the very footscraper that did it! Did you stop there? No. Some people would have been quite satisfied, but not you. Your intellect went on working. 'Let me find a door-mat,' says you to yourself, 'and my theory is proved!' And of course you found your door-mat. You're so clever, I believe you could find anything you liked. 'Now,' says you, 'that door exists, that is clear. Nothing remains to be done but to find it!' Well, I've read about that sort of thing in books, but I've never come across it before in real life. You ought to go where you'll be properly appreciated. You're simply wasted here, among us stupid fellows. If I only had your brain, Ratty—"

"But as you haven't," interrupted the Rat, rather unkindly, "I suppose you're going to sit on the snow all night and TALK. Get up at once and hang on to that bell-pull you see there, and ring hard, as hard as you can, while I hammer!"

While the Rat attacked the door with his stick, the Mole sprang up at the bell-pull, clutched it and swung there, both feet well off the ground, and from quite a long way off they could faintly hear a deep-toned bell respond.

CHAPTER 4

Mr. Badger

They waited patiently for what seemed a very long time, stamping in the snow to keep their feet warm. At last they heard the sound of slow shuffling footsteps approaching the door from the inside. It seemed, as the Mole remarked to the Rat, like someone walking in bedroom slippers that were too large for him. This was intelligent of Mole, because that was exactly what it was.

There was the sound of a lock being unlocked, and the door opened a few inches, enough to show a long snout and a pair of sleepy blinking eyes.

"Now, the VERY next time this happens," said a gruff and suspicious voice, "I shall be exceedingly angry. Who is it THIS time, disturbing me on such a night? Speak up!"

"Oh, Badger," cried the Rat, "let us in,

please. It's me, Rat, and my friend Mole, and we've lost our way in the snow."

"What, Ratty, my dear little man!" exclaimed the Badger, in quite a different voice. "Come along in, both of you, at once. Why, you must be half-dead with cold. I never! Lost in the snow! And in the Wild Wood, too, and at this time of night! But come in with you."

The two animals tumbled over each other in their eagerness to get inside, and heard the door shut behind them with great joy and relief.

The Badger, who wore a long bathrobe, and whose slippers were indeed very large and well-worn, carried a candlestick in his paw. It looked as if he had been on his way to bed when the bell had rung. He looked kindly down on them and patted both their heads. "This is not the sort of night for small animals to be out," he said in a fatherly tone. "I'm afraid you've been up to some of your pranks again, Ratty. But come along; come into the kitchen. There's a first-rate fire there, and supper and everything."

He shuffled on in front of them, carrying the light, and they followed him (nudging each other in a happy, hopeful sort of way) down a long, gloomy passage. They passed into a sort of central hall, out of which they could dimly see other long, mysterious, tunnel-like passages branching. But there were doors in the hall as well—stout oaken doors. The Badger flung open one of these, and they found themselves in the glow and warmth of a large fire-lit kitchen.

The floor was well-worn red brick, and on the wide hearth burned a log fire. A couple of high-backed benches beside the fire provided seating. In the middle of the room stood a long plain wooden table, with more benches down each side. At one end of it, where an armchair stood pushed back, were spread the remains of the Badger's plain but ample supper. Rows of spotless plates winked from shelves at the far end of the room, and from the rafters overhead hung hams, bundles of dried herbs, nets of onions, and baskets of eggs. It seemed a place where heroes could feast after victory, where weary harvesters could line up by the dozens along the table to eat and sing, or where two or three friends of simple tastes could sit about and eat and smoke and talk in comfort.

The kindly Badger seated them to toast themselves at the fire, and reminded them to remove their wet coats and boots. Then he fetched them bathrobes and slippers, and he himself washed the Mole's shin with warm water and bandaged the cut until the whole thing was just as good as new, if not better. The storm-driven animals relaxed in the comforting firelight, warm and dry at last, with weary legs propped up in front of them, and the clink of plates being arranged on the table behind them. It seemed to them that the cold and frightening Wild Wood was miles and miles away, and all that they had suffered was just a dream.

When at last they were thoroughly toasted, the Badger called them to the table. They had felt pretty hungry before, but when they actually saw the supper that was spread out for them, they could hardly decide what to attack first. Conversation was impossible for a long time; when it was slowly resumed, they still spoke with their mouths full. The Badger did not mind that sort of thing at all, nor care if their elbows were on the table, or if everybody spoke at once. As he did not go into Society himself, he had gotten the idea that these things didn't really matter. (We know of course that he was wrong, because they do matter very much, though it would take too long to explain why.) He sat in his armchair at the head of the table, and nodded gravely as the animals told their story. He did not seem

surprised or shocked at anything, and he never said, "I told you so." The Mole began to feel very friendly toward him.

When supper was really finished at last, and each animal felt that his belly was now as full as was decently safe, they gathered round the glowing embers of the great wood fire, and thought how jolly it was to be sitting up SO late, and SO independent, and SO well-fed. After they had chatted for a time about things in general, the Badger said heartily, "Now then! Tell me the news from your part of the world. How's old Toad getting on?"

"Oh, from bad to worse," said the Rat

gravely, while the Mole, basking in the firelight, tried to look properly mournful. "Another smash-up only last week, and a bad one. You see, he insists on driving himself, and he's hopeless at it. If he'd only employ a decent, steady, well-trained animal, pay him good wages, and leave everything to him, he'd be all right. But no; he's convinced he's a natural-born driver, and nobody can teach him anything."

"How many has he had?" inquired the Badger gloomily.

"Smashes, or cars?" asked the Rat. "Oh, well, after all, it's the same thing with Toad. This is the seventh."

"He's been in the hospital three times," put in the Mole. "And as for the fines he's had to pay, it's simply awful to think of."

"Yes, and that's part of the trouble," continued the Rat. "Toad's rich, we all know, but not THAT rich. And he's a hopelessly bad driver, and pays no attention to law and order. He'll be killed or ruined sooner or later. Badger! We're his friends—shouldn't we do something?"

The Badger thought hard. "Now look here!" he said at last, rather severely; "of course you know I can't do anything NOW?"

His two friends agreed, quite understanding. No animal, according to the rules of animal etiquette, is ever expected to do anything strenuous, or heroic, or even moderately active during the winter. All are sleepy—some are actually asleep. All are weather-bound, more or less, and all are resting from their hard-working days and nights.

"Very well then!" continued the Badger. "BUT, when the winter is over, and the nights are shorter . . . well, then," went on the Badger, "we'll take Toad seriously in hand. We'll put up with none of his nonsense. We'll bring him back to reason, by force if need be. We'll MAKE him be a sensible Toad. We'll—you're asleep, Rat!"

"Not me!" said the Rat, waking up with a jerk.

"He's been asleep two or three times since supper," said the Mole, laughing. He himself was feeling quite wakeful and even lively, though he didn't know why. The reason was, of course, that he was by nature an underground animal, so Badger's house suited him very well. The Rat, on the other hand, slept every night in a bedroom whose windows opened onto a breezy river, and he naturally found the atmosphere still and oppressive.

"Well, it's time we were all in bed," said the Badger, getting up and fetching candlesticks. "Come along, you two, and I'll show you your quarters. And take your time tomorrow morning—breakfast at any hour you please!"

He led the two animals to a long chamber. The Badger's winter stores took up half the room—piles of apples, turnips, and potatoes; baskets full of nuts; and jars of honey. But the two little white beds looked soft and inviting, and the sheets on them were clean and smelled beautifully of lavender. The Mole and the Water Rat, shaking off their clothes in some thirty seconds, fell between those sheets in great joy and contentment.

In accordance with the kindly Badger's invitation, the two tired animals came down to breakfast very late next morning. They found a bright fire burning in the kitchen, and two young hedgehogs sitting on a bench at the table, eating oatmeal out of wooden bowls. The hedgehogs dropped their spoons, rose to their feet, and bowed their heads respectfully as the two entered.

"There, sit down, sit down," said the Rat pleasantly, "and go on with your oatmeal. Where have you youngsters come from? Lost your way in the snow, I suppose?"

"Yes, sir," said the older of the two hedgehogs. "Me and little Billy here, we was trying to find our way to school—mother said we must go, even with the weather so bad—and of course we got lost, sir, and Billy he got frightened and started up crying, being young and faint-hearted. And at last we found Mr. Badger's back door, and we knocked, sir, for Mr. Badger he's a kindhearted gentleman, as everyone knows—"

"I understand," said the Rat, cutting himself some bacon, while the Mole dropped some eggs into a saucepan. "And what's the weather like outside? You needn't call me 'sir' quite so much," he added.

"Oh, terrible bad, sir, terrible deep the snow is," said the hedgehog. "No getting out for the likes of you gentlemen today."

"Where's Mr. Badger?" inquired the Mole, as he warmed the coffeepot before the fire.

"In his study, sir," replied the hedgehog, "and he said he was going to be particular busy this morning, and under no circumstances was he to be disturbed."

This explanation, of course, was understood by everyone present. The animals knew very well what Badger was doing. Having eaten a hearty breakfast, he had gone to his study and settled himself in one armchair with his legs up on another and a red cotton handkerchief over his face, and was being "busy" in the usual way for this time of year.

The front doorbell clanged loudly. The Rat, who was very greasy with buttered toast, sent Billy, the smaller hedgehog, to see who it was. There was a sound of much stamping in the hall, and presently Billy returned with the Otter, who threw himself on the Rat with an embrace and a shout of affectionate greeting.

"Get off!" spluttered the Rat, with his mouth full.

"I thought I should find you here," said the Otter cheerfully. "They were all very alarmed along Riverbank when I arrived this morning. They said Rat hadn't been home all night, nor Mole either, and something dreadful must have happened. But I knew that when people were in any fix they mostly went to Badger, or else Badger got to know of it somehow, so I came straight here, through the Wild Wood and the snow!

"About halfway here, I came upon a rabbit sitting on a stump, cleaning his silly face with his paws. He was a pretty scared animal when I crept up behind him and placed a paw on his shoulder. I had to smack his head once or twice to get any sense from him at all. At last I managed to learn that Mole had been seen in the Wild Wood last night. It was the talk of the burrows, he said, how Mole was in a bad fix; how he had lost his way, and 'They' were up and out hunting, and were chasing him round and round.

"'Then why didn't any of you DO something?' I asked him. 'Even if you aren't blessed with brains, there are hundreds and hundreds of you, big, stout fellows, with your burrows running in all directions. You could have taken him in and made him safe and comfortable.' But he just said, 'What, US? DO something? Us rabbits?' So I smacked him again and left him. At any rate, I had learned something; and if I had had the luck to meet any of 'Them' I would have learned something more—or THEY would."

"Weren't you at all—er—nervous?" asked the Mole, remembering some of yesterday's terror at the mention of the Wild Wood.

"Nervous?" The Otter showed his gleaming white teeth as he laughed. "I'd give 'em nerves if any of them tried anything with me. Here, Mole, fry me some slices of ham, like the good little chap you are. I'm frightfully hungry, and I've got a great deal of gossip to tell Ratty here. Haven't seen him for an age."

So the good-natured Mole, having cut some slices of ham, put the hedgehogs to work frying it, and returned to his own breakfast. Meanwhile the Otter and the Rat eagerly talked river-talk, which runs on as endlessly as the babbling river itself.

A plate of fried ham had just been cleared and sent back for more, when the Badger entered, yawning and rubbing his eyes. He greeted them all in his quiet, simple way. "It must be nearly lunch time," he remarked to the Otter. "Better stop and have it with us. You must be hungry on this cold morning."

"Wonderful idea!" replied the Otter, winking at the Mole. "The sight of these young hedgehogs stuffing themselves with fried ham makes me feel positively famished."

The hedgehogs, who were just beginning to feel hungry again after their porridge, and after working so hard at their cooking, looked timidly up at Mr. Badger, but were too shy to say anything.

"Here, you two youngsters, be off home to your mother," said the Badger kindly. "I'll send someone with you to show you the way."

He gave them each a quarter and a pat on the head, and they went off feeling happy and grateful.

Presently they all sat down to lunch together. The Mole found himself next to Mr. Badger, and, as the other two were still deep in their river-gossip, he took the opportunity to tell Badger how much he liked his home. "Once you're underground," he said, "you know exactly where you are. Nothing can happen to you, and nothing can get at you. You're entirely your own master, and you don't have to consult anybody or mind what they say. Things go on overhead, and you don't bother about 'em. When you want to, up you go, and there the things are, waiting for you."

The Badger beamed at him. "That's exactly what I say," he replied. "There's no security, or peace and tranquility, except underground. And then, if your ideas get larger and you want to expand your house—why, a dig and a scrape, and there you are! No builders, no contractors, no remarks by fellows looking over your wall, and, above all, no WEATHER. Look at Rat, now. When he gets a couple of feet of floodwater, he's got to move into hired rooms. That's uncomfortable, inconvenient, and horribly expensive. Or take Toad. I have nothing to say against Toad Hall; it's the best house in these parts. But suppose a fire breaks out—where's Toad? Suppose tiles blow off, or walls sink or crack, or windows get broken—where's Toad? Supposing the rooms are cold and drafty—I HATE a draft myself—where's Toad? No, up and outdoors is good enough to roam about in. But underground to come back to at last—that's my idea of HOME."

The Mole agreed heartily, and the Badger as a result got very friendly with him. "When lunch is over," he said, "I'll take you all around this little place of mine. I can see you'll appreciate it. You understand what domestic architecture ought to be, you do."

And so after lunch, when the other two had settled themselves into the chimney-corner and started a heated argument on the subject of eels, the Badger lighted a lantern and showed Mole all around his marvelous underground home. Mole found everything exactly to his taste, and admired it all, and he and Badger found themselves becoming very good friends. Badger began speaking of his neighbors aboveground when he said, "The Wild Wood is pretty well populated by now with all the usual lot—good, bad, and indifferent. I name no names. It takes all sorts to make a world. But I imagine you know something about them yourself by this time."

"I do indeed," said the Mole, with a slight shiver.

"Well, well," said the Badger, patting him on the shoulder, "it was your first experience with them, you see. They're not so bad really;

we must all live and let live. But I'll pass the word around tomorrow, and I think you'll have no further trouble. Any friend of MINE can walk where he likes in this country, or I'll know the reason why!"

When they got back to the kitchen again, they found the Rat walking up and down, very restless. The underground atmosphere was getting on his nerves. He really seemed to be afraid that the river would run away if he wasn't there to look after it. So he had his overcoat on, and his pistols thrust into his belt again. "Come along, Mole," he said anxiously, as soon as he caught sight of them. "We must get off while it's daylight. We don't want to spend another night in the Wild Wood."

"It'll be all right, my fine fellow," said the Otter. "I'm coming with you, and I know every path blindfolded. If there's a head that needs to be punched, you can confidently rely upon me to punch it."

"Don't worry, Ratty," added the Badger. "My tunnels run further than you think, and I've got shortcuts to the edge of the wood in several directions, though I don't care for everybody to know about them. You shall leave by one of them."

The Rat was still anxious to be off, so the

Badger picked up his lantern again. They passed through a damp and airless tunnel that wound and dipped for what seemed to be miles. At last, daylight began to show itself through the tangled growth overhanging the mouth of the passage. The Badger, bidding them a hasty goodbye, pushed them hurriedly through the opening. He then made everything look as natural as possible again by covering it with vines, brushwood, and dead leaves, and retreated.

They found themselves standing on the very edge of the Wild Wood. Rocks and brambles and tree roots lay behind them, confusedly heaped and tangled. In front was a great space of quiet fields, hemmed by hedges black against the snow, and, far ahead, a glint of the dear old river. The Otter, knowing all the paths, took charge here, and they made a beeline for a distant fence. Pausing there a moment and looking back, they saw the whole mass of the Wild Wood. It seemed dense, menacing, and grim in its vast white surroundings. Then they turned and headed swiftly for home, for firelight and the river's cheerful voice.

As he hurried along, eagerly anticipating the moment when he would be at home again, the Mole realized something about himself. Others might enjoy the danger and conflict that were part of Nature in the rough. But he preferred the pleasant places. They held enough adventure, in their way, to last for a lifetime.

CHAPTER 5

Home Sweet Home

The sheep ran huddling together against the fence, snorting steam into the frosty air, as the two animals hurried by, chatting and laughing. They were returning after a long day's adventure with Otter, hunting and exploring along small streams that flowed into their own River. Now the shadows of the short winter day were closing in on them, and they had still some distance to go. As they plodded along, they had heard the sheep and had headed toward them. Now, leading from the sheep-pen, they found a beaten track that made walking easier. They were responding to that small voice (which all animals carry inside them) that said unmistakably, "Yes, quite right; THIS way leads home!"

"It looks as if we are coming to a village," said the Mole somewhat doubtfully, slowing down. The track had become a path, then a lane, and it now turned into an actual road. The animals did not generally care for villages.

"Oh, don't worry!" said the Rat. "At this season of the year they're all safe indoors by this time, sitting round the fire—men, women, and children, dogs and cats and all. We shall slip through all right, without any bother. If you like, we can even have a look at them through their windows, and see what they're doing."

The mid-December nightfall had already overtaken the little village as they approached it through a thin fall of powdery snow. There was little visible except the squares of dusky orange-red on either side of the street, where the firelight or lamplight of each cottage flowed through the windows. Few of the windows had blinds, so the animals could observe the residents gathered around the tea table, absorbed in handiwork, or talking and laughing. Moving from one window to another, the two spectators felt a little homesick as they watched a cat being stroked, a sleepy child picked up and carried off to bed, or a tired man stretch and knock out his pipe on the end of a smoldering log.

Once they were beyond the village, they

could smell the friendly fields through the darkness again. They were finally on the home stretch, and they plodded along silently, each thinking his own thoughts. The Mole's were primarily about supper, as it had been a long day, and he was hungry. He was following obediently behind the Rat, leaving the guidance up to him. As for the Rat, he was walking a little way ahead, his shoulders humped, his eyes fixed on the straight gray road in front of him. So he did not notice poor Mole when the call suddenly reached him, shocking him like a jolt of electricity.

We others, who have lost so much of our physical senses, do not even have the right words to describe how an animal communicates with his surroundings. We have only the word "smell," for instance, to include the whole range of delicate thrills which murmur in the nose of the animal night and day—summoning, warning, exciting, repelling. It was one of these mysterious calls from out of the darkness that had suddenly reached Mole, making him tingle all over, even while he could not clearly remember why. He stopped dead in his tracks, his nose searching here and there in its efforts to recapture that fine thread, that tiny current that had so strongly moved him. A moment later he had caught it again, and with it this time came a flood of memories.

Home! That was what they meant, those soft touches carried through the air, those invisible little hands pulling and tugging at him! It must be quite close by him, his old home that he had hurriedly abandoned that day when he first found the river! And now it was sending out its messengers to capture him and bring him in. Since his escape on that bright morning, he had hardly given it a thought. He had been too absorbed in his new life, with all its pleasures, its surprises, its fresh and captivating experiences. Now, with a rush of old memories, how clearly it stood before him in the darkness! His home was shabby, true; and small and poorly furnished—and yet it was HIS, the home he had made for himself, the home he had been so happy to get back to after his day's work. And the home had been happy with him, too, evidently, and was missing him, and wanted him back. It was telling him so through his nose, reminding him that it was there, and wanted him.

The call was clear, the summons was plain. He must obey it instantly, and go. "Ratty!" he called, full of joyful excitement. "Stop! Come back! I need you, quick!"

"Oh, COME along, Mole, do!" replied the Rat cheerfully, still plodding along.

"PLEASE stop, Ratty!" pleaded the poor Mole. "You don't understand! It's my home, my old home! I've just come across the smell of it, and it's close by here, really quite close. And I MUST go to it, I must, I must! Oh, come back, Ratty! Please, please come back!"

By this time the Rat was very far ahead, too far to hear clearly what the Mole was saying—too far to catch the pain in his voice. And he was worried about the weather, for he too could smell something—something suspiciously like approaching heavy snow.

"Mole, we mustn't stop now, really!" he called back. "We'll come for it tomorrow, whatever it is. But I don't dare stop now—it's late, and the snow's coming on again, and I'm not sure of the way. I need your nose, Mole, so come on quick, like a good fellow!" And the Rat went forward on his way without waiting for an answer.

Poor Mole stood alone in the road, his heart torn in two, and a big sob gathering somewhere low down inside him. But even under such a test, his loyalty to his friend stood firm. Never for a moment did he dream of abandoning him. Meanwhile, the scents from his old home pleaded and whispered.

He did not dare stay longer within their reach. With a wrench that tore his very heartstrings he turned away and followed submissively in the Rat's tracks, while faint, thin little smells, following after his retreating nose, reproached him for his new friendship and his heartless forgetfulness.

With an effort he caught up to the unsuspecting Rat, who began chattering cheerfully about what they would do when they got back, and how jolly a fire in the parlor would be, and what a big supper he meant to eat. He never noticed his companion's silence and distressful state of mind. At last, however, when they had gone quite a long way and were passing some tree stumps, he stopped and said kindly, "Look here, Mole old chap, you seem dead tired. There's no talk left in you, and your feet are dragging like lead. We'll sit down here for a minute and rest. The snow has held off so far, and the worst part of our journey is over."

The Mole sank forlornly onto a tree stump and tried to control himself, for he felt it surely coming. The sob he had fought with so long refused to be beaten. Up it forced its way into the air, and then another, and another, and others thick and fast. Poor Mole gave up the struggle, and cried freely and helplessly.

The Rat, astonished and dismayed at Mole's grief, did not dare to speak for a while. At last he said, very quietly and sympathetically, "What is it, old fellow? Whatever can be the matter? Tell me, and let me see if I can help."

Poor Mole found it difficult to get any words out between the upheavals of his chest. At last he sobbed out, brokenly, "I know it's a—shabby, dingy little place, not like—your cozy quarters—or Toad's beautiful hall—or Badger's great house—but it was my own little home—and I was fond of it—and I went away and forgot all about it—and then I smelled it suddenly on the road, when I called and you wouldn't listen, Rat—and everything came back to me with a rush—and I WANTED it!—Oh dear, oh dear!—and when you wouldn't turn back, Ratty—I had to leave it, though I was smelling it all the time. I thought my heart would break. We might have just gone and had one look at it, Ratty—only one look—it was close by—but you wouldn't turn back, Ratty, you wouldn't turn back! Oh dear, oh dear!"

Remembering brought fresh waves of sorrow, and sobs again took charge of him, preventing further speech.

The Rat stared straight in front of him, saying nothing, only patting Mole gently on the shoulder. After a time he muttered gloomily, "I see it all now! What a PIG I have been! A pig—that's me! Just a pig—a plain pig!"

He waited until Mole's sobs became gradually less stormy and more rhythmic; he waited until his sniffs were frequent and sobs only occasional. Then he rose from his seat, and, saying carelessly, "Well, now we'd really better be getting on, old chap!" he set off up the road again, back the same way they had come.

"Wherever are you (hic) going (hic), Ratty?" cried the tearful Mole, looking up in alarm.

"We're going to find that home of yours, old fellow," replied the Rat pleasantly; "so you had better come along, for it will take some finding, and we shall need your nose."

"Oh, come back, Ratty, do!" cried the Mole, getting up and hurrying after him. "It's no good, I tell you! It's too late, and too dark, and the place is too far off, and the snow's coming! And—and I never meant to let you know I was feeling that way about it—it was all an accident and a mistake! And think of Riverbank, and your supper!"

"Hang Riverbank, and supper too!" said the Rat heartily. "I tell you, I'm going to find this place now, if I stay out all night. So cheer up, old chap, and take my arm, and we'll soon be back there again."

Still snuffling, pleading, and reluctant, Mole allowed himself to be dragged back along the road by his bossy companion, who talked and joked steadily in an effort to cheer Mole up and make the weary way seem shorter. When finally it seemed to the Rat that they must be near the right part of the road, he said, "Now, no more talking. Use your nose, and set your mind to it."

They moved on in silence for some little way. Suddenly the Rat was aware (through his arm that was linked through Mole's) of a faint sort of electric thrill that was passing down that animal's body. Instantly he dropped the arm, fell back a step, and waited, all attention.

The signals were coming through!

Mole stood rigid a moment, while his uplifted nose, quivering slightly, felt the air.

Then a short, quick run forward—a false start—stop—another try—and then a slow, steady, confident advance.

The Rat, very excited, kept close to his heels as the Mole moved like a sleepwalker across a dry ditch, through a hedge, and over a field that seemed trackless and bare in the faint starlight.

Suddenly, without warning, he dived. But the Rat was on the alert, and promptly followed him down the tunnel to which his nose had faithfully led him.

It was tight and airless, and the earthy smell was strong, and it seemed a long time to Rat before the passage ended and he could stand straight, stretching and shaking himself. The Mole struck a match, and by its light the Rat saw that they were standing in an open space, neatly swept underfoot, and directly facing them was Mole's little front door, with "Mole End" painted over the bell-pull at the side.

Mole took down a lantern from a nail and lit it, and the Rat, looking round him, saw that they were in a sort of courtyard. A garden bench stood on one side of the door. On the walls hung wire baskets with ferns in them, alternating with shelves holding little statues, including one of Queen Victoria. Down one side of the courtyard ran a bowling alley, with benches along it and little wooden tables marked with rings that hinted at beer mugs. In the middle was a small round pond containing goldfish and surrounded by a cockleshell border.

Mole's face beamed at the sight of all these objects, so dear to him, and he hurried Rat through the door. Then he lit a lamp in the hall, and took one glance around his old home. He saw the dust lying thick on everything; saw the cheerless, deserted look of the long-neglected house, its narrow dimensions, its worn and shabby contents—and collapsed again on a hall-chair, his nose to his paws. "Oh Ratty!" he cried dismally, "why did I do it? Why did I bring you to this poor, cold little place, on a night like this, when you might have been at Riverbank by this time, toasting your toes before a blazing fire!"

The Rat paid no attention to this at all. He was running here and there, opening doors, inspecting rooms and cupboards, and lighting lamps and candles and sticking them up everywhere. “What a splendid little house this is!” he called out cheerily. “So compact! So well planned! A place for everything, and everything in its place! We’ll make a jolly night of it. The first thing we want is a good fire. I’ll see to that—I always know where to find things. So this is the parlor? Marvelous! Was this your own idea, those little sleeping bunks in the wall? Wonderful! Now, I’ll fetch the wood and the coals, and you get a duster, Mole, and try and neaten things up a bit. Bustle about, old chap!”

Encouraged by his spirited companion, the Mole roused himself and dusted and polished with energy, while the Rat, running to and fro with armfuls of fuel, soon had a cheerful blaze roaring up the chimney. He called the Mole to come and warm himself, but Mole promptly had another fit of the blues, dropping down on a couch in dark despair and burying his face in his duster. “Rat,” he moaned, “how about your supper, you poor, cold, hungry, weary animal? I’ve nothing to give you—nothing— not a crumb!”

“What a fellow you are for giving up!” said the Rat reproachfully. “Why, only just now I saw a can opener on the kitchen dresser, and everybody knows that means there are sardines somewhere in the neighborhood.

Rouse yourself! Pull yourself together, and come with me and look."

They did go and look, hunting through every cupboard and emptying every drawer. The result was not so very depressing after all, though of course it might have been better—a tin of sardines, a box of crackers, nearly full, and a German sausage wrapped in silver paper.

"There's a banquet for you!" observed the Rat, as he arranged the table. "I know some animals who would give their ears to be sitting down to supper with us tonight!"

"No bread!" groaned the Mole sadly. "No butter, no—"

"No caviar, no champagne!" continued the Rat, grinning. "And that reminds me—what's that little door at the end of the hallway? Your cellar, of course! There's every luxury in this house! Just you wait a minute."

He headed for the cellar door, and soon reappeared, somewhat dusty, with a bottle of beer in each paw and another under each arm, "You really are a self-indulgent beggar, Mole," he observed. "You deny yourself nothing. This is really the jolliest little place I ever was in. Now, wherever did you pick up those pictures on the wall? They make the place look so home-like, they do. No wonder you're so fond of it, Mole. Tell me all about it, and how you came to make it what it is."

Then the Rat busied himself fetching plates, and knives and forks, and mustard. The Mole (his chest still heaving with the stress of his recent emotion) told—somewhat shyly at first, but more freely as he warmed to his subject—how this was planned, and how that was thought out, and how this was an inheritance from an aunt, and that was a wonderful bargain, and this other thing was bought only after saving money for ever so long. He began feeling so much better that he took a lamp and showed off each possession, explaining it in detail, and quite forgetting about supper. Rat was desperately hungry but tried to conceal it, saying, "wonderful," and "most remarkable," when Mole seemed to expect a response.

At last the Rat succeeded in luring him to the table, and had just got seriously to work with the can opener when sounds were heard from the courtyard outside—sounds like the scuffling of small feet in the gravel and a confused murmur of tiny voices. Bits of sentences reached them—"Now, all in a line—hold the lantern up a bit, Tommy—clear your throats first—no coughing after I say one, two, three—Where's young Bill?—Here, come on, we're all a-waiting—"

"What's that?" inquired the Rat, pausing in his labors.

"I think it must be the field mice," replied the Mole, with a touch of pride in his manner. "They go round singing carols at this time of the year. They're quite a tradition in these parts. And they never pass me over—they come to Mole End last of all, and I used to give them hot drinks, and supper too sometimes, when I could afford it. It will be like old times to hear them again."

"Let's have a look at them!" cried the Rat, jumping up and running to the door.

It was a pretty sight that met their eyes when they flung the door open. In the courtyard, lit by the dim rays of a lantern, some eight or ten little field mice stood in a semicircle.

Red knit scarves wound round their throats, their forepaws were thrust deep into their pockets, and their feet danced a little for warmth. With bright beady eyes they glanced shyly at each other, giggling a little. As the door opened, one of the older ones that carried the lantern was just saying, "Now then, one, two, three!" and at once their shrill little voices rose in the air, singing a little carol that their forefathers had composed.

When their voices ceased, the singers, bashful but smiling, exchanged glances, and silence followed. "Very well sung, boys!" cried the Rat heartily. "And now come in, all of you, and warm yourselves by the fire, and have something hot!"

"Yes, come along, field mice," cried the Mole eagerly. "This is just like old times! Shut the door after you. Pull up that bench to the fire. Now, you just wait a minute, while we—oh, Ratty!" he cried in despair, plumping down on a seat, nearly in tears again. "Whatever are we doing? We have nothing to give them!"

"You leave all that to me," said the masterful Rat. "Here, you with the lantern! Come over here. I want to talk to you. Now, tell me, are there any shops open at this hour of the night?"

"Why, certainly, sir," replied the field mouse respectfully. "At this time of the year our shops keep open very late."

"Then look here!" said the Rat. "You go off at once, you and your lantern, and you get me—"

Here much muttered conversation followed, and the Mole only heard bits of it, such as—"Be sure it's fresh!—no, a pound of that will do—be sure to get Buggins's, for I won't have any other brand—no, only the best—if you can't get it there, try somewhere else—yes, of course, homemade, no canned stuff—well then, do the best you can!" Finally, there was a chink of coins passing from paw to paw, the field mouse was given a large basket for his purchases, and off he hurried.

The rest of the field mice, perched in a row on the bench with their small legs swinging, thoroughly enjoyed the fire, and toasted their chilly feet until they tingled. The Mole tried to get them to talk, but failed, so he made each of them recite the names of his numerous brothers who were too young to go out caroling this year, but looked forward to getting their parents' permission soon.

The Rat, meanwhile, was busy examining the label on a bottle. "Sensible Mole! The very best thing! Now we shall be able to mull some ale. Get the things ready, Mole, while I draw the corks."

It did not take long to prepare the brew, and soon every field mouse was sipping and coughing and choking (for a little mulled ale goes a long way) and wiping his eyes and laughing and forgetting he had ever been cold in all his life.

"They perform plays too, these fellows," the Mole explained to the Rat. "Make them up all by themselves, and act them out. And very well they do it, too! They gave us a fine one last year, about a field mouse who was captured at sea by a Barbary pirate, and forced to row in a galley ship, and when he escaped and got home again, his ladylove had become a nun. Here, you! You were in it, I remember. Get up and recite a bit."

The field mouse he spoke to got up, giggled shyly, looked round the room, and remained absolutely tongue-tied. His comrades cheered him on, Mole coaxed and encouraged him, and the Rat went so far as to shake him by the shoulders, but nothing could overcome his stage fright. They were all busy with him when the latch clicked, the door opened, and the field mouse with the lantern reappeared, staggering under the weight of his basket.

There was no more talk of acting once the very real and solid contents of the basket had tumbled out on the table. Under the leadership of Rat, everybody was set to do something or to fetch something. In a very few minutes supper was ready, and Mole, as he looked on from his seat, saw a once-empty table set thick with savory comforts. He saw his little friends' faces brighten and beam as they enjoyed the wonderful food, and then he let himself loose—for he was starving indeed—on the goodies so magically provided. As they ate, they talked of old times, and the field mice told him the local gossip, and answered as well as they could the hundred questions he had to ask them. The Rat said almost nothing, only taking care that each guest had what he wanted, and plenty of it, and that Mole had no trouble or anxiety about anything.

They went off at last, very grateful and with many best wishes of the season, with their jacket pockets stuffed with treats for the small brothers and sisters at home. When the door had closed on the last of them and the light of their lanterns had died away, Mole and Rat threw another log on the fire, drew up their chairs, brewed themselves a nightcap of mulled ale, and discussed the events of the long day. At last the Rat, with a tremendous yawn, said, "Mole, old chap, I'm ready to drop. That's your own bunk over on that side? Very well, then, I'll take this. What a wonderful little house this is! Everything so handy!"

He climbed into his bunk, rolled himself up in the blankets, and was asleep immediately.

The weary Mole was also glad to turn in without delay, and soon had his head on his pillow. But before he closed his eyes he let them wander around his old room for a few moments. Everything was mellow in the glow of the firelight. The room was full of familiar and friendly things—things which had long been a part of him, and now smilingly welcomed him back. He was now in exactly the frame of mind that the kindly Rat had tried to bring about in him. He saw clearly how plain and simple it all was. But he saw as well how much it all meant to him, and the value of such an anchor in one's existence. He did not at all want to abandon his new life, to turn his back on sun and air and all they offered him in order to creep home and stay here. The world aboveground was too strong; it called to him still, even down here, and he knew he must return to the larger stage. But it was good to think he had this to come back to;

this place which was all his own, these things which were so glad to see him again, and could always be counted upon for the same simple welcome.

CHAPTER 6

Mr. Toad

It was a bright morning in the early part of summer. The hot sun seemed to be pulling everything green and bushy and spiky up out of the earth and toward it, as if by strings. The Mole and the Water Rat had been up since dawn, very busy on matters connected with boats and the opening of the boating season. They had been painting and varnishing, mending paddles, repairing cushions, hunting for missing boat hooks, and so on. Now they were finishing breakfast in their little parlor and discussing their plans for the day, when a heavy knock sounded at the door.

"Bother!" said the Rat, with egg all over him. "See who it is, Mole, like a good chap, since you've finished."

The Mole went to answer the knock, and the Rat heard him utter a cry of surprise.

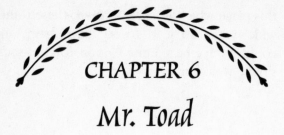

Then he flung the parlor door open, and announced with much importance, "Mr. Badger!"

The Badger strode heavily into the room, and stood looking at the two animals with a serious expression. The Rat let his egg spoon fall on the tablecloth, and sat open-mouthed.

"The hour has come!" said the Badger at last, very solemnly.

"What hour?" asked the Rat uneasily, glancing at the clock on the mantelpiece.

"WHOSE hour, you should say," replied the Badger. "Why, Toad's hour! The hour of Toad! I said I would take him in hand as soon as the winter was over, and I'm going to take him in hand today!"

"Toad's hour, of course!" cried the Mole delightedly. "Hooray! I remember now! WE'LL teach him to be a sensible Toad!"

"I learned last night, from a trustworthy source, that this very morning," continued the Badger, taking an armchair, "another new and exceptionally powerful motorcar will arrive at Toad Hall. At this very moment, perhaps, Toad is busy dressing himself in those hideous driving clothes which transform him from a (comparatively) good-looking Toad into an Object which throws any decent-minded animal into a violent fit. We must be up and doing, before it is too late. You two animals will accompany me instantly to Toad Hall, and we shall perform our work of rescue."

"Right you are!" cried the Rat, jumping up. "We'll rescue the poor unhappy animal! We'll convert him! He'll be the most converted Toad that ever was before we're done with him!"

They set off up the road on their mission of mercy, Badger leading the way. They reached the driveway of Toad Hall to find, as the Badger had predicted, a large, shiny new motorcar, painted bright red (Toad's favorite color). As they neared the house the door was flung open, and Mr. Toad, wearing goggles, cap, and an enormous overcoat, came swaggering down the steps, pulling on his driving gloves.

"Hello, there!" he cried cheerfully on catching sight of them. "You're just in time to come with me for a jolly—to come for a jolly—for a—er—jolly—"

His hearty greeting faltered as he noticed the stern looks on the faces of his silent friends, and his invitation remained unfinished.

The Badger strode up the steps. "Take him inside," he said sternly to his companions. Then, as Toad was hustled through the door, struggling and protesting, he turned to the servant in charge of the new motorcar.

"I'm afraid you won't be wanted today," he said. "Mr. Toad has changed his mind. He will not require the car. You needn't wait." Then he followed the others inside and shut the door.

"Now then!" he said to the Toad, when the four of them stood together in the Hall, "first of all, take those ridiculous things off!"

"I won't!" replied Toad, with great spirit. "What is the meaning of this outrage? I demand an explanation."

"Take them off him, you two," ordered the Badger briefly.

They had to lay Toad on the floor, kicking and calling them all sorts of names, before they could get to work properly. Then the Rat sat on him, and the Mole got his driving clothes off him bit by bit, and they stood him up on his legs again. A good deal of his blustering spirit seemed to have evaporated with the removal of his fine costume. Now that he was merely Toad, and no longer the Terror of the Highway, he giggled feebly and looked from one to the other appealingly.

"You knew it must come to this, sooner or later, Toad," the Badger explained severely. "You've ignored all the warnings we've given you. You've squandered the money your father left you, and you're getting us animals a bad name with your furious driving and your smashes and your run-ins with the police. Independence is all very well, but we animals never allow our friends to make fools of themselves beyond a certain limit, and that limit is reached. Now, you're a good fellow in many respects, and I don't want to be too hard on you. I'll make one more effort to bring you to reason. You will come with me into the library, and there you will hear some facts about yourself."

He took Toad firmly by the arm, led him into the library, and closed the door behind them.

"THAT'S no good!" said the Rat, contempt in his voice. "TALKING to Toad will never cure him. He'll SAY anything."

They made themselves comfortable in armchairs and waited patiently. Through the closed door they could hear the continuous drone of the Badger's voice, rising and falling in waves. Presently they heard the sermon punctuated here and there by noisy sobs, evidently coming from Toad. He was a soft-hearted and affectionate fellow, very easily converted—for the time being—to any point of view.

After three-quarters of an hour the door

opened, and the Badger reappeared, solemnly leading by the paw a very limp and dejected Toad. His skin hung baggily about him, his legs wobbled, and his cheeks were stained by the tears called forth by the Badger's moving comments.

"Sit down there, Toad," said the Badger kindly, pointing to a chair. "My friends," he went on, "I am pleased to inform you that Toad has seen the error of his ways. He is truly sorry for his misguided conduct in the past, and he has decided to give up motorcars forever. I have his solemn promise on that."

"That is very good news," said the Mole gravely.

"Very good news indeed," observed the Rat doubtfully, "if only—"

He was looking very hard at Toad as he said this, and could not help thinking there was something resembling a twinkle in that animal's still sorrowful eyes.

"There's only one more thing to be done," continued the satisfied Badger. "Toad, I want you solemnly to repeat, before your friends here, what you admitted to me in the library just now. First, are you sorry for what you've done, and do you see the folly of it all?"

There was a long, long pause. Toad

looked desperately this way and that, while the other animals waited in grave silence. At last he spoke.

"No!" he said. "I'm NOT sorry. And it wasn't folly at all! It was glorious!"

"What?" cried the Badger, greatly scandalized. "You backsliding animal, didn't you tell me just now, in there—"

"Oh, yes, yes, in THERE," said Toad impatiently. "I would have said anything in THERE. You're so eloquent, dear Badger, and so moving, and so convincing, and put all your points so frightfully well. But I've been thinking it over, and I find that I'm not a bit sorry or repentant really, so it's no earthly good saying I am. Is it?"

"Then you don't promise," said the Badger, "never to touch a motorcar again?"

"Certainly not!" replied Toad emphatically. "On the contrary, I faithfully promise that the very first motorcar I see, poop-poop! off I go in it!"

"Told you so, didn't I?" observed the Rat to the Mole.

"Very well, then," said the Badger firmly, rising to his feet. "Since you won't yield to persuasion, we'll see what force can do. I feared it would come to this. You've often asked us three to come and stay with you,

Toad, in this handsome house of yours. Well, now we're going to. When we've converted you to a proper point of view we may leave, but not before. Take him upstairs, you two, and lock him in his bedroom, while we arrange matters between ourselves."

"It's for your own good, Toady, you know," said the Rat kindly, as Toad, kicking and struggling, was hauled up the stairs by his two faithful friends. "Think what fun we shall all have together, just as we used to, when you've quite got over this— this painful attack of yours!"

"We'll take care of everything until you're well, Toad," said the Mole, "and we'll see your money isn't wasted, as it has been."

"No more of those regrettable incidents with the police, Toad," said the Rat, as they threw him into his bedroom.

"And no more weeks in the hospital, being ordered about by nurses, Toad," added the Mole, turning the key.

They descended the stairs, Toad shouting abuse at them through the keyhole, and the three friends met in conference.

"It's going to be a difficult business," said the Badger, sighing. "I've never seen Toad so determined. However, we will see it out. He must never be left unguarded for an instant.

We shall have to take turns being with him, until the poison has worked itself out of his system."

They arranged watches accordingly. Each animal took turns sleeping in Toad's room at night, and they divided the day up between them. At first Toad was very difficult to be with. He would often arrange bedroom chairs to resemble a motorcar. He would then crouch on the first of them, bent forward and staring fixedly ahead, making uncouth and ghastly noises. When the high point was reached he would turn a complete somersault, then lie flat amid the ruins of the chairs, apparently completely satisfied for the moment. As time passed, however, these painful seizures grew less frequent, and his friends tried to distract his mind with fresh topics. But his interest in other matters did not revive, and he grew languid and depressed.

One fine morning the Rat, whose turn it was to go on duty, went upstairs to relieve Badger, who was planning a long walk round the woods. "Toad's still in bed," he told the Rat, outside the door. "I can't get much out of him, except, 'Oh, leave me alone, I want nothing,' and so on. Now, you look out, Rat! When Toad's being quiet and submissive, then he's at his most sneaky. There's sure to be something up. Well, now, I must be off."

"How are you today, old chap?" inquired the Rat cheerfully, as he approached Toad's bedside.

He had to wait some minutes for an answer. At last a feeble voice replied, "Thank you so much, dear Ratty! So good of you to inquire! But first tell me how you are yourself, and the excellent Mole?"

"Oh, WE'RE all right," replied the Rat. "Mole," he added carelessly, "is going out for a run around with Badger. They'll be out till lunchtime, so you and I will spend a pleasant morning together, and I'll do my best to amuse you. Now jump up, like a good fellow, and don't lie moping on a fine morning like this!"

"Dear, kind Rat," murmured Toad, "how little you understand my condition, and how unable I am to 'jump up' now—if ever! But do not trouble about me. I hate being a burden to my friends, and I do not expect to be one much longer. Indeed, I almost hope not."

"Well, I hope not, too," said the Rat heartily. "You've been a fine bother to us, and I'm glad to hear it's going to stop. And in weather like this, and the boating season just beginning! It's too bad of you, Toad! It isn't the trouble we mind, but you're making us miss such an awful lot."

"I'm afraid it IS the trouble you mind, though," replied the Toad languidly. "I can quite understand it. It's natural enough. You're tired of bothering about me. I mustn't ask you to do anything further. I'm a nuisance, I know."

"You are, indeed," said the Rat. "But I tell you, I'd go to any trouble for you, if only you'd be a sensible animal."

"If I believed that, Ratty," murmured Toad, more feebly than ever, "then I would beg you—for the last time, probably—to go to the village as quickly as possible and fetch the doctor. But don't you bother. Perhaps we should just let nature take its course."

"Why, what do you want a doctor for?" asked the Rat, coming closer and examining him. He certainly lay very still and flat, and his voice was weak.

"Surely you have noticed lately . . ." murmured Toad. "But, no—why should you? Noticing things is only a trouble. Tomorrow, indeed, you may be saying to yourself, 'Oh, if only I had noticed sooner! If only I had done something!' But no; it's a trouble. Never mind—forget that I asked."

"Look here, old man," said the Rat, beginning to get rather alarmed, "of course I'll fetch a doctor for you, if you really think you need him. But you can hardly be bad enough for that. Let's talk about something else."

"I fear, dear friend," said Toad, with a sad smile, "that 'talk' can do little in a case like this—or doctors either, for that matter. Still, one must have hope. And, by the way, while you are at it—I HATE to give you additional trouble, but just happened to think of it—would you mind asking my lawyer to stop by? It would be a convenience to me, and there are moments when one must face disagreeable tasks, no matter how exhausted one is!"

"A lawyer! Oh, he must be really bad!" the frightened Rat said to himself as he hurried from the room. He did not forget, however, to lock the door carefully behind him.

Outside, he stopped to think. The other two were far away, and he had no one to talk to.

"It's best to be on the safe side," he said at last. "I've known Toad to imagine himself frightfully sick before, without the slightest reason, but I've never heard him ask for a lawyer! If there's nothing the matter, the doctor will tell him he's an ass, and cheer him up.

That will do some good. I'd better humor him and go; it won't take very long." So he ran off to the village on his errand of mercy.

The Toad, who had hopped lightly out of bed as soon as he heard the key turned in the lock, watched him eagerly from the window until he was out of sight. Then, laughing heartily, he dressed as quickly as possible in the most stylish suit he could lay his hands on, and he filled his pockets with cash. Next, knotting the sheets from his bed together and tying one end of the improvised rope around the windowsill, he scrambled out, sliding to the ground. Taking the opposite direction to the Rat, he marched off lightheartedly, whistling a merry tune.

It was a gloomy lunch for Rat when the Badger and the Mole finally returned, and he had to face them with his pitiful and unconvincing story. The Badger's brutal remarks may be imagined, and therefore passed over. But it was painful to the Rat that even the Mole, although he took his friend's side as far as possible, could not help saying, "You've been a bit of a sucker this time, Ratty! Toad, too, of all animals!"

"He did it awfully well," said the crestfallen Rat.

"He did YOU awfully well!" rejoined the

Badger hotly. "However, talking won't mend matters. He's got away for the time, that's certain. The worst of it is, he'll be so conceited with what he'll think is his cleverness that he may do anything. One comfort is, we're free now, and needn't waste any more of our time playing prison guard. But we'd better continue to sleep at Toad Hall for a while longer. Toad may be brought back at any moment—on a stretcher, or between two policemen."

So spoke the Badger, not knowing how much troubled water was to run under bridges before Toad should be safe again in his ancestral Hall.

Meanwhile, Toad, happy and irresponsible, was walking briskly along the main road, some miles from home. At first he had taken little paths, and crossed many fields, and changed his course several times. But now that he was feeling safe from recapture, the sun smiled brightly on him, and all Nature joined the song of self-praise that his own heart was singing. He almost danced along the road in self-satisfaction.

"That was a smart piece of work!" he remarked to himself, chuckling. "Brain against brute force—and brain came out on the top, as it's bound to do. Poor old Ratty!

My! Won't he catch it when the Badger gets back! A worthy fellow, Ratty, with many good qualities, but very little intelligence and absolutely no education. I must take him in hand some day, and see if I can make something of him."

Filled with conceited thoughts such as these he strode along until he reached a little town. There the sign of "The Red Lion Inn," reminded him that he had not breakfasted that day, and that he was exceedingly hungry. He marched into the Inn, ordered the best lunch that could be provided at short notice, and sat down to eat it in the coffee room.

He was about halfway through his meal when an all too familiar sound made him jump, then start trembling all over. The poop-poop! drew nearer and nearer. Then the car could be heard turning into the inn yard and coming to a stop, and Toad had to hold on to the leg of the table to hide his emotion. Presently the people from the car streamed into the coffee room. They were hungry, talkative, and cheerful, chatting on about their experiences of the morning and the merits of the automobile that had brought them along so well. Toad listened eagerly, all ears. At last he could stand it no longer. He slipped out of the room quietly, paid his bill at the bar, and

as soon as he got outside wandered round quietly to the inn yard. "There cannot be any harm," he said to himself, "in just LOOKING at it!"

The car stood in the middle of the yard, quite alone. The stable hands were all at their dinner. Toad walked slowly around it, inspecting, criticizing, thinking deeply.

"I wonder," he said to himself presently, "I wonder if this sort of car STARTS easily?"

The next moment, hardly knowing how it happened, he found he had taken hold of the handle and was turning it. As the familiar sound broke forth, the old passion seized Toad and completely mastered him, body and soul. As if in a dream he found himself seated in the driver's seat; as if in a dream, he swung the car around the yard and out through the archway; and, as if in a dream, all sense of right and wrong, all fear of consequences, seemed temporarily suspended. He increased his speed, and as the car devoured the street and leaped forth on the highway through the open country, he was only conscious that he was Toad once more, Toad at his best and highest, Toad the terror, the Lord of the lone trail, before whom all must give way or be smitten into nothingness . . .

"In my opinion," observed the Judge cheerfully, "the ONLY question facing us in this otherwise very clear case is this: How can we sufficiently punish this scoundrel who we see cowering before us? Let me see: he has been found guilty, first, of stealing a valuable motorcar; secondly, of reckless driving; and, thirdly, of great rudeness to the local police. Mr. Clerk, will you tell us, please, what is the very stiffest penalty we can impose for each of these offenses?"

The Clerk scratched his nose with his pen. "Some people would say," he observed, "that stealing the motorcar was the worst offense, and so it is. But talking back to the police carries the severest penalty, and so it ought. Suppose you were to say twelve months for the theft, which is mild; and three years for the furious driving, which is lenient; and fifteen years for the rudeness, which was a pretty bad sort of rudeness, judging by what we've heard from the witness box, even if you only believe one-tenth part of what you heard. Those figures, if added together correctly, come up to nineteen years—"

"First-rate!" said the Judge.

"So you had better make twenty years to be on the safe side," concluded the Clerk.

"An excellent suggestion!" said the Judge approvingly. "Prisoner! Pull yourself together and try and stand up straight. It's going to be twenty years for you this time. And mind, if you appear before us again, we shall deal with you very seriously!"

Then the officers of the law fell upon the helpless Toad. They loaded him with chains and dragged him from the Court House, shrieking, praying, and protesting. Across the marketplace, the playful townspeople joined in with jeers, carrots, and insults. On and on he was dragged until they reached the door of the grimmest dungeon in the land. There at last they paused, where an ancient jailer sat fingering a bunch of mighty keys.

"Wake up there!" said the sergeant of police, taking off his helmet and wiping his forehead. "Rouse yourself, old loon, and take charge of this vile Toad. He is a criminal of the worst kind. Guard him with all your skill. And don't forget, graybeard, that if he should escape, you'll answer for it—and a pox on both of you!"

The jailer nodded grimly, laying his withered hand on the shoulder of the miserable Toad. The rusty key creaked in the lock, the great door clanged behind them. Toad was a helpless prisoner in the remotest dungeon of the best-guarded castle in all the length and breadth of Merry England.

CHAPTER 7

The Piper at the Gates of Dawn

Though it was past ten o'clock at night, a bit of light remained in the sky. The suffocating heat of the afternoon was rolling away under the cool fingers of the short midsummer night. Mole lay stretched on the bank, still panting from the fierce heat of the day, waiting for his friend to return. He had been out on the river, leaving the Water Rat free to visit Otter, and he had come back to find the house dark and deserted. It was still too hot to stay indoors, so he lay on the cool grass, thinking over the pleasures of the past day.

He presently heard the Rat's light footstep approaching over the parched grass. "Oh, the blessed coolness!" Rat said, and sat down, gazing thoughtfully into the river.

"You stayed for supper, then?" said the Mole.

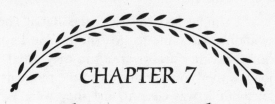

"I simply had to," said the Rat. "They wouldn't allow me to go before. You know how kind they always are. And they acted as jolly as they could, right up to the moment I left. But it was clear to me they were very unhappy, although they tried to hide it. Mole, I'm afraid they're in trouble. Little Portly is missing again. You know how fond his father is of him."

"Oh, that child!" said the Mole lightly. "Well, suppose he is missing; why worry about it? He's always straying off and getting lost, and turning up again. No harm ever comes to him. Someone always brings him back again all right. Why, we've found him ourselves, miles from home, perfectly safe and cheerful!"

"Yes, but this time it's more serious," said the Rat gravely. "He's been missing for days now, and the Otters have hunted everywhere, without finding the slightest trace. They've asked every animal for miles around, and no one knows anything. Otter told me that young Portly hasn't learned to swim very well yet, and I can see he's worried about the dam. There's a lot of water coming down still, considering the time of the year, and the place has always fascinated the child. And then there are—well, traps and things. Poor old man—

he was going to spend the night watching by the ford. You know the place where animals used to cross the river, before they built the bridge?"

"I know it well," said the Mole. "But why would Otter watch there?"

"Well, that's where he gave Portly his first swimming lesson," continued the Rat. "And it was there that young Portly caught his first fish. The child loves the spot, so Otter goes there every night and watches—just in case, you know, just in case!"

They were silent for a time, both thinking of the same thing—about the lonely, heartsick animal crouched by the ford, watching and waiting the long night through.

"Well," said the Rat presently, "I suppose we ought to be going in." But he didn't move.

"Rat," said the Mole, "I can't go to sleep and do nothing. Let's get the boat out, and paddle up stream. The moon will be up in an hour or so, and then we will search as well as we can. It will be better than going to bed and doing NOTHING."

"Just what I was thinking myself," said the Rat. "It's not the sort of night for sleep anyhow, and daybreak is not so very far off. We may pick up some news of him from early risers as we go along."

They got the boat out, and the Rat took the oars. Out in midstream there was a clear, narrow track of light, but wherever shadows fell the water seemed as solid as the riverbank, and the Mole had to steer very carefully. Although the night was dark and deserted, it was full of small noises—song and chatter and rustling, reminding them that a busy little nighttime community was up and about. The water's own noises, too, were more noticeable than by day. Its gurglings and slapping against the side of the boat seemed unexpected and near at hand.

Fastening their boat to a willow, the friends landed in the silent, silver kingdom of the night, and patiently explored the hedges, the hollow trees, the ditches and dry waterways. Boarding their boat again and crossing over, they worked their way slowly up the stream. The moon, serene in a cloudless sky, did what she could to help them search. But at last her hour came and she sank earthward reluctantly, and dark mystery once more spread over field and river.

Then something changed. The horizon became clearer, and the fields and trees came more into sight. A bird piped suddenly, then was still; a light breeze sprang up and set the reeds rustling. Rat, who was in the front of the boat while Mole rowed, sat up suddenly and listened with a passionate intensity. Mole looked at him curiously.

"It's gone!" sighed the Rat, sinking back in his seat again. "So beautiful and strange! I almost wish I had never heard it. Now I feel a sort of painful longing, and nothing seems worthwhile except hearing that sound once more. There it is again!" he cried, alert once more. Entranced, he was silent for a long time, spellbound.

"Now it is passing—I am losing it," he said. "Oh Mole! How beautiful it is! What a joyous sound! I never dreamed of such music. Row on, Mole, row! It is calling us!"

The Mole was greatly puzzled, but he obeyed. "I hear nothing myself," he said, "but the wind in the reeds and trees."

The Rat didn't answer; he didn't seem to hear. Entranced, trembling, he was enchanted by this divine new thing that had caught him up. It rocked and cradled him, and he was a powerless but happy infant in its grasp.

In silence, Mole rowed steadily on. Soon they came to a point where the river divided, and a long backwater branched off to one side. With a slight movement of his head, Rat directed Mole to take the backwater. The light grew brighter, and now they could see the color of the flowers that dotted the water's edge.

"Clearer and nearer still," cried the Rat joyously. "Now you must surely hear it! At last—I see you do!"

Breathless, the Mole stopped rowing as the glorious notes of the pipe reached him, caught him up, and possessed him completely. He saw the tears on his comrade's cheeks, and bowed his head in understanding. For a few moments they stayed there, and then the clear, demanding melody moved him to action, and he began to row again. The light grew steadily stronger, but no birds sang as they usually do at the approach of dawn. Except for the heavenly music, all was still.

On either side of them, as they glided onward, the rich meadow grass seemed impossibly fresh and green. The roses had never looked so vivid, the meadow flowers so sweet smelling. Then the murmur of the approaching dam began to fill the air, and they felt sure that they were nearing the end of their expedition. Ahead of them, in the middle of the stream, lay a small island, bordered thickly with willows, silver birches, and alders.

Slowly, but with no doubt or hesitation, the two animals moored their boat at the flowery edge of the island. In silence they landed, and pushed through the blossom and scented grass that led up to the level ground. There they found a little lawn of a marvelous green, set round with crab apple and wild cherry trees.

"This is the place of my dream song, the place the music played to me," whispered the Rat, as if in a trance. "Here, in this holy place, surely we shall find Him!"

Then suddenly the Mole felt a great awe fall upon him, an awe that turned his muscles to water, bowed his head, and rooted his feet to the ground. It was no panicky terror—indeed he felt wonderfully at peace and happy—but it meant that some great Being was very, very near. With difficulty he turned to look for his friend, and saw him at his side, trembling violently. There was utter silence in the bird-filled branches around them, and still the light grew and grew.

He would not have dared to raise his eyes, but although the piping had stopped, the summons seemed more urgent than ever. He could not refuse, even if Death himself was waiting to strike him. Trembling, he raised his humble head. And there, in that utter clearness of the coming dawn, he looked in the very eyes of the Friend and Helper. He saw

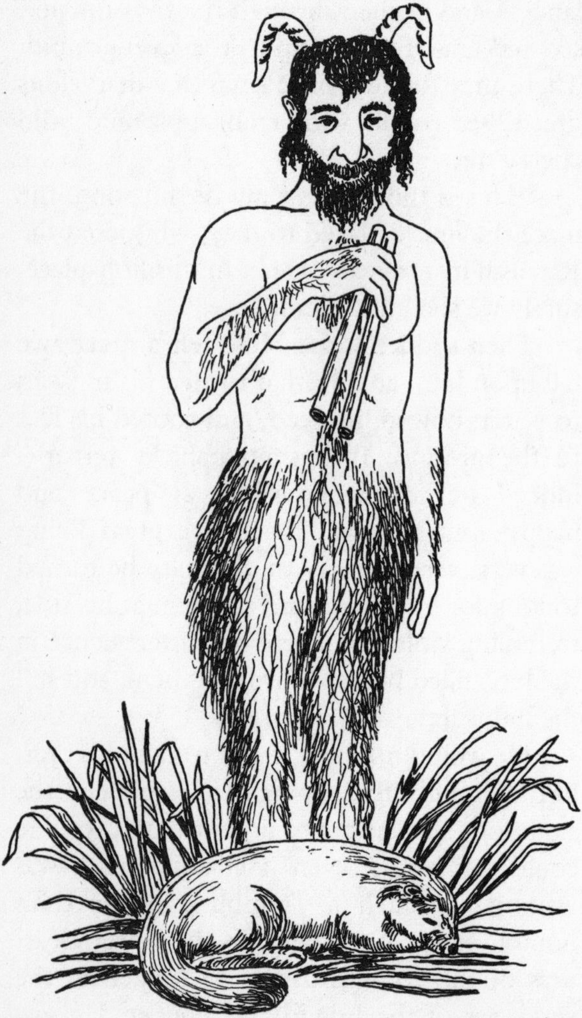

the backward sweep of the curved horns, gleaming in the growing daylight. He saw the stern, hooked nose between the kindly eyes that looked down on them humorously, while the bearded mouth broke into a half-smile. He saw the rippling muscles on the arm that lay across the broad chest, the long graceful hand still holding the pan pipes. He saw the splendid curves of the shaggy limbs. Last of all, nestling between His very hooves, sleeping soundly, Mole saw the little, round, pudgy, childish form of the baby otter.

"Rat!" he whispered, shaking. "Are you afraid?"

"Afraid?" murmured the Rat, his eyes shining with love. "Afraid of HIM? Oh, never, never! And yet—and yet— oh, Mole, I am afraid!"

Then the two animals, crouching to the earth, bowed their heads and worshipped.

Suddenly and magnificently, the sun's broad golden disk appeared over the horizon facing them. The first rays hit the animals full in the eyes and dazzled them. When they were able to look once more, the Vision had vanished, and the air was full of the carol of birds greeting the dawn.

They stared blankly, a feeling of misery setting in as they realized what they had seen and what they had lost. Just then, a playful little breeze danced up from the surface of the water and blew lightly in their faces. With its soft touch came instant forgetfulness. For this is the last, best gift that kindly Pan gives to those to whom he has revealed himself: the gift of oblivion. Otherwise the awe-inspiring memory would remain and grow, and overshadow joy and pleasure, and spoil the afterlives of little animals helped out of difficulties.

Mole rubbed his eyes and stared at Rat, who was looking around him in a puzzled sort of way. "I beg your pardon; what did you say, Rat?" he asked.

"I was only saying," said Rat slowly, "that this is the right sort of place to find him—and look! There he is, the little fellow!" And with a cry of delight he ran toward the slumbering Portly.

But Mole stood still a moment, held in thought. Like one wakened suddenly from a beautiful dream, he struggled to recall it, but could capture nothing but a dim sense of its beauty. Then that, too, faded away, and Mole shook his head sadly and followed the Rat.

Portly woke up with a joyous squeak, and wriggled with pleasure at the sight of his father's friends, who had played with him so often in the past. In a moment, however, his face grew blank, and he began hunting about with a pleading whine. Like a child that has fallen happily asleep in its mother's arms, and wakes to find itself alone in a strange place, Portly searched the island doggedly. He finally gave up and sat down, crying bitterly.

The Mole ran quickly to comfort the little animal; but Rat, lingering, looked long and doubtfully at hoof-marks deep in the grass.

"Some . . . great . . . animal . . . has been here," he murmured slowly. He stood thinking and thinking, his mind strangely stirred.

"Come along, Rat!" called the Mole. "Think of poor Otter, waiting up there by the ford!"

Portly was soon comforted by the promise of a ride on the river in Mr. Rat's boat, and the two animals placed him securely between them, and paddled off down the backwater. The sun was fully up by now, and hot; birds sang lustily, and flowers nodded from the banks, but somehow (or so the animals thought) with less richness and blaze of color than they had seen quite recently somewhere—they wondered where.

Once they reached the main river, they turned upstream, toward the point where they knew their friend was keeping his lonely watch. As they drew near the familiar ford, the

Mole took the boat to the bank. There they lifted Portly out and set him on the towpath, headed him in the right direction, gave him a friendly farewell pat on the back, and shoved out into midstream. They watched the little animal as he waddled along the path; watched until they saw his muzzle suddenly lift and his waddle break into a clumsy run. Looking up the river, they could see Otter leap up, tense and rigid, from out of the shallows where he crouched patiently. They heard his amazed and joyous bark as he bounded up through the bushes and on to the path. Then the Mole, with a strong pull on one oar, swung the boat around and let the stream bear them downstream.

"I feel strangely tired, Rat," said the Mole, leaning wearily over his oars as the boat drifted. "You'll say it's because we've been up all night, but that's nothing. We're up plenty of nights, at this time of the year. No; I feel as if I had been through something very exciting and rather terrible. And yet nothing particular has happened."

"Or something very surprising and splendid and beautiful," murmured the Rat, leaning back and closing his eyes. "I feel just as you do, Mole; simply dead tired. It's lucky we've got the current with us, to take us home. Isn't it jolly to feel the sun again, soaking into your bones! And listen to the wind in the reeds!"

"It's like music—far away music," said the Mole, nodding sleepily.

"That's what I was thinking," murmured the Rat. "It's like dance music—but with words in it, too, sometimes. I catch them now and then, but then it's only music again, and then nothing but the wind in the reeds."

"You hear better than I," said the Mole sadly. "I cannot catch the words."

"Let me try and tell you them," said the Rat softly, his eyes still closed. "Now it is turning into words again—faint but clear." He began to repeat them softly:

So that the awe won't dwell
And turn your play to fret
You shall look on my power at the
helping hour
But then you shall forget!

So paws aren't cut and torn
I spring the trap that is set
As I loose the snare you may glimpse
me there
But surely you shall forget!

"Row nearer, Mole, nearer to the reeds!" Rat said. "It is hard to catch, and grows fainter each minute. No, it's no good—I've lost it. All there is is the noise of the wind."

"But what do the words mean?" asked the Mole.

"I do not know," said the Rat. "Ah! now they're back again, full and clear! This time, it is the real thing—unmistakable, simple, perfect—"

"Well, let's hear it, then," said the Mole, after he had waited patiently for a few minutes, half-dozing in the hot sun.

But no answer came. He looked, and understood the silence. With a smile of much happiness, and a listening look still lingering on his face, the weary Rat was fast asleep.

CHAPTER 8

Toad's Adventures

When Toad found himself trapped in a dark, foul-smelling dungeon, and knew that a medieval fortress lay between him and the outer world of sunshine and open roads where he had recently been so happy, he threw himself on the floor and shed bitter tears.

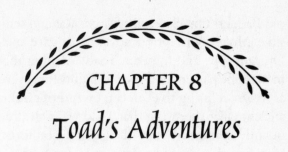

"This is the end of everything!" he said. "At least it is the end of the Toad, which is the same thing—popular, handsome Toad; rich, hospitable Toad; Toad, so careless and debonair! How can I hope to be set free again, after stealing such a handsome motor-car in such an outrageous manner! And for raining down such rich, imaginative insults upon so many fat, red-faced policemen!" (Here his sobs choked him.) "Stupid animal that I was," he continued, "now I must languish in this dungeon, until my friends have forgotten the very name of Toad! Oh, wise old Badger! Oh, clever, intelligent Rat and sensible Mole! What good advice you gave me! Oh, unhappy and forsaken Toad!" And in this manner he passed his days and nights for several weeks, refusing to even eat, even though the ancient jailer (knowing that Toad was rich) frequently reminded him that many comforts, even luxuries, could be delivered—for a price.

Now the jailer had a daughter, a pleasant, goodhearted girl, who assisted her father in his duties. She was particularly fond of animals, and kept a canary, several spotted mice, and a restless squirrel. This kindhearted girl said to her father one day, "Father, I can't bear to see that poor beast so unhappy, and getting so thin! You must let me care for him. You know how fond I am of animals. I'll make him eat from my hand, and sit up, and do all sorts of things."

Her father replied that she could do what she liked with him. He was tired of Toad and his sulking. So that day she went on her errand of mercy, and knocked at the door of Toad's cell.

"Now, cheer up, Toad," she said, "and sit up and dry your eyes and be a sensible animal. And do try and eat a bit of dinner. See, I've brought you some of mine, hot from the oven!"

It was a lovely casserole, and its fragrance filled the narrow cell. The aroma reached Toad's nose as he lay in his misery on the floor, and made him think for a moment that perhaps life was not such an empty thing after all. But still he wailed, and kicked his legs, and refused to be comforted. So the wise girl left for a bit, but, of course, a good deal of the smell of hot casserole remained behind too. Toad, between his sobs, sniffed that scent, and gradually began to think new and inspiring thoughts. He thought about chivalry, and poetry, and brave deeds still to be done, and of the comforting clink of dishes on the table at Toad Hall, and the scrape of chair legs on the floor as everyone pulled himself close to dinner. He began to think about his friends, and how they would surely be able to do something; of lawyers, and how he should have hired a few; and finally, he thought of his own great cleverness, and all that he was capable of if he only gave his mind to it. By then, the cure was almost complete.

When the girl returned some hours later, she carried a tray. On it was a cup of fragrant tea, and a plate piled with very hot buttered toast, cut thick, very brown on both sides, with the butter running through the holes in it in great golden drops, like honey from the honeycomb. The smell of that buttered toast simply talked to Toad. It talked of warm kitchens, of breakfasts on bright frosty mornings, of cozy parlor firesides on winter evenings, of the purring of contented cats, and the twitter of sleepy canaries. Toad sat up and dried his eyes, sipped his tea and munched his toast. Soon he began talking freely about himself, and the house he lived in, and his life there, and how important he was, and how highly his friends thought of him.

The jailer's daughter saw that the topic was doing him as much good as the tea, and encouraged him to go on.

"Tell me about Toad Hall," she said. "It sounds beautiful."

"Toad Hall," said the Toad proudly, "is a very unique gentleman's residence. It dates in part from the fourteenth century, but possesses every modern convenience. Up-to-date plumbing, five minutes from the church, post office, and golf course. Suitable for—"

"Bless you," said the girl, laughing, "I don't want to *buy* it. Tell me something real about it. But first wait until I fetch you some more tea and toast."

She left, and presently returned with fresh supplies. Toad, pitching into the toast with great appetite, told her about the boathouse, and the fish pond, and the old walled kitchen garden, and the stables, and the pigeon house, and the henhouse, and the dairy, and the washhouse, and the banquet hall, and the fun they had there when the other animals were gathered round the table and Toad was singing songs and telling stories. Then she wanted to know about his animal friends, and was very interested in all he had to tell her about them and how they lived, and what they did to pass their time. Of course, she did not say she was fond of animals as PETS, because she had the sense to see that Toad would be extremely offended. By the time she said good night, Toad was his old confident, self-satisfied self. He sang a little song or two (of the sort he used to sing at his dinner parties), curled himself up in the straw, and had an excellent night's rest.

They had many interesting talks together after that, as the dreary days went on. The jailer's daughter grew very sorry for Toad, and thought it was a great shame that a poor little animal should be locked up for what seemed to her a trivial offense. Toad, of course, was so vain that he thought she was romantically interested in him. He could not help regretting that he was so much higher born than the lowly girl, for she was pretty, and obviously admired him very much.

One morning the girl was very thoughtful, and did not seem to Toad to be paying proper attention to his witty sayings and sparkling comments.

"Toad," she said finally, "just listen, please. I have an aunt who is a washerwoman."

"There, there," said Toad, graciously, "never mind; think no more about it. I have several aunts who OUGHT to be washerwomen."

"Do be quiet a minute, Toad," said the girl. "You talk too much, that's your worst fault, and I'm trying to think. As I said, I have an aunt who is a washerwoman. She does the washing for all the prisoners here. She picks up the washing on Monday morning, and brings it back on Friday evening. This is a Thursday. Now, this is what occurs to me: you're very rich—at least you're always telling me so—and she's very poor. A few dollars wouldn't make any difference to you, and it would mean a lot to her. I think if she were properly approached, she could arrange to let you have her dress and bonnet and so on, and you could escape from the prison disguised as the official washerwoman. You're very alike in many respects—particularly in your figure."

"We're NOT," said the Toad indignantly. "I have a very elegant figure—for what I am."

"So does my aunt," replied the girl, "for what SHE is. But have it your way. You horrid, proud, ungrateful animal. I'm just trying to help you!"

"Yes, yes, that's all right; thank you very much indeed," said the Toad hurriedly. "But look here! You surely wouldn't expect Mr. Toad of Toad Hall to go about the country disguised as a washerwoman!"

"Then you can stay here in prison, as fine Mr. Toad," replied the girl with much spirit.

Honest Toad was always ready to admit when he was wrong. "You are a good, kind, clever girl," he said, "and I am indeed a proud and a stupid toad. Would you please be so kind as to introduce me to your worthy aunt? I am certain that the excellent lady and I will be able to come to a satisfactory agreement."

Next evening the girl brought her aunt into Toad's cell, carrying his laundry wrapped up in a towel. The old lady had been prepared beforehand, and the sight of a pile of money that Toad had thoughtfully placed on the table in full view made further discussion unnecessary. In return for his cash, Toad received a cotton print gown, an apron, a shawl, and a faded black bonnet. All that the old lady asked was that she should be tied up, gagged, and dumped in a corner. By doing this, she explained, she hoped to keep her job, in spite of the suspicious appearance of things.

Toad was delighted with the suggestion. It would add to his reputation for being a desperate and dangerous fellow. He happily helped the jailer's daughter make her aunt appear the victim of a crime.

"Now it's your turn, Toad," said the girl. "Take off your vest and coat; you're fat enough as it is."

Shaking with laughter, she proceeded to button him into the cotton gown, arranged the shawl, and tied the strings of the bonnet under his chin.

"You could be her twin," she giggled. "Now, goodbye, Toad, and good luck. Go straight down the way you came up. If any of the men tease you, as they probably will, you can answer back a bit. But remember that you're a respectable widow woman, and don't lose your good reputation."

Feeling very scared, but acting as normal as possible, Toad cautiously began his dangerous undertaking. He was soon pleased to find how easy everything was. The washerwoman's squat figure in its familiar cotton dress seemed like a passport for every locked door and grim gateway. Even when he hesitated, uncertain which turn to take, the guard at the next gate (anxious to be off on break) called to him to come along and not keep him waiting all night. The teasing from the guards was actually the worst danger he encountered, for Toad was a dignified animal. He managed to keep his temper, though, and joked back as he thought the washerwoman might.

It seemed hours before he crossed the last courtyard. He had to dodge the outspread arms of the last guard, who pleaded jokingly for one farewell embrace. But at last he heard the gate in the great outer door click behind him, felt the fresh air of the outer world, and knew that he was free!

Dizzy with success, he walked quickly toward the lights of the town. He did not know what he should do next, but he was certain that he must leave the neighborhood where the washerwoman was so well-known.

As he walked along thinking, he noticed some red and green lights a little way off, and the sound of the puffing and snorting of engines. "Aha!" he thought, "this is a piece of luck! A train station is exactly what I need."

He hurried to the station, looked at a schedule, and found that a train was leaving in the direction of his home in half an hour.

"More luck!" said Toad, his spirits rising rapidly, and went off to buy his ticket.

He asked for a ticket, and automatically reached his hand to where his jacket pocket, and money, should have been. But here the cotton dress, which had been so helpful to this point, failed him. In a sort of nightmare he searched, while other travelers muttered impatiently behind him. To his horror he remembered that he had left not only his jacket back in his prison cell, but also his money, keys, watch, matches—everything, in fact, that made his life worth living.

In his misery he turned to the ticket seller and said in his usual, proud, Mr. Toad-like manner, "Look here! I find I've left my purse at home. Just give me that ticket, will you, and I'll send the money to you tomorrow. I'm well-known in these parts."

The clerk stared at him and the dirty black bonnet a moment, and then laughed. "I don't doubt that you're well-known in these parts," he said, "if you've tried that trick often. Step away from the window, madam, and let the other passengers by."

Baffled and despairing, Toad wandered blindly down the platform, tears trickling down each side of his nose. It was hard to be so close to safety, yet stopped by the want of a few miserable dollars. Very soon his jailers would discover his escape. He would be caught, loaded with chains, and dragged back to prison and a diet of bread and water. He would be treated twice as badly as before, and what sarcastic remarks the girl would make! What could he do? Could he squeeze under the seat of a train car? He had seen schoolboys try this trick, when they had spent the traveling money provided by their parents on other, better things. As he worried, he found himself near the engine, which was being oiled by its driver, a burly man with an oil can in one hand and a towel in the other.

"Hello, mother!" said the engine driver, "what's the trouble? You don't look particularly cheerful."

"Oh, sir!" said Toad, starting to cry all over again. "I am a poor unhappy washerwoman, and I've lost all my money, and can't pay for a ticket, and I must get home tonight somehow, and I don't know what to do. Oh dear, oh dear!"

"That's a shame," said the engine driver reflectively. "Lost your money, and can't get home. And you've got some kids, too, waiting for you, I imagine?"

"Any number of them," sobbed Toad. "And they'll be hungry—and playing with matches—and knocking lamps over, and quarrelling, and generally making trouble."

"Well, I'll tell you what I'll do," said the good engine driver. "You're a washerwoman, says you. And I'm an engine driver, as you can see, and that's a terribly dirty job. I use up more shirts than I can count, until my wife is sick to death of washing them. If you'll wash a few shirts for me when you get home, and send them back to me, I'll give you a ride on my engine. It's against regulations, of course, but we're not so very strict in these out-of-the-way parts."

The Toad's misery turned into delight as he eagerly scrambled up into the cab of the engine. Of course, he had never washed a shirt in his life, and didn't plan to try. But he thought, "When I get safely home to Toad Hall, I will send the engine driver enough to pay for plenty of washing, and that will be just as good or better."

The train moved out of the station. As the speed increased, the Toad could see real fields, and trees, and hedges, and cows, and horses, all flying past him. He thought how every minute was bringing him closer to Toad Hall, and his friends, and money to jingle in his pocket, and a soft bed to sleep in, and good things to eat. At the thought of his adventures and great cleverness he began to skip up and down, shouting and singing bits of song. This astonished the engine driver, who had met washerwomen before, but never one at all like this.

They had covered many miles, and Toad was already planning what he would have for supper, when he noticed the engine driver leaning out of his cab with a puzzled expression on his face. He commented, "This is very strange. We're the last train running in this direction tonight, yet I could swear that I hear another one following us!"

Toad stopped his dancing at once. He became grave and depressed, and a dull pain in his lower back made him want to sit down and try desperately not to think of the possibilities.

By this time the moon was shining brightly, and the engine driver could see behind them for a long distance.

Presently he called out, "I can see it clearly now! It is an engine, on our rails, coming along very fast. We are being pursued!"

The miserable Toad, crouching on the floor, tried hard to think about other things, with a complete lack of success.

"They are catching up with us fast!" cried the engine driver. "And the engine is crowded with people! It's . . . it's . . . policemen, and what looks to me like plain clothes detectives. They're waving revolvers and walking sticks and shouting, 'Stop, stop, stop!' "

Then Toad fell on his knees on the dusty floor and, raising his clasped paws, cried, "Save me, save me, dear kind Mr. Engine driver, and I will confess everything! I am not the simple washerwoman I seem to be! I have no children waiting for me, innocent or otherwise! I am a toad—the well-known and popular Mr. Toad. I have just escaped (by great daring and cleverness) from a dreadful dungeon into which my enemies had flung me. If those fellows on that engine recapture me, it will be chains and bread-and-water and misery once more for poor, unhappy, innocent Toad!"

The engine driver looked at him very sternly, and said, "Now tell the truth; what were you put in prison for?"

"It was nothing very much," said poor Toad, blushing deeply. "I only borrowed a motorcar while the owners were at lunch. They weren't using it, after all. I didn't mean to steal it, really; but people—especially judges—take such harsh views of thoughtless and high-spirited actions."

The engine driver looked very grave and said, "I fear you have been a wicked toad, and

I probably ought to hand you over to the law. But you are in trouble, so I will not desert you. I don't like motorcars, for one thing, and I don't like being ordered about by policemen when I'm on my own engine, for another. And I'm softhearted at the sight of an animal in tears. So cheer up, Toad! I'll do my best, and we may beat them yet!"

Shoveling furiously, they piled more coal into the engine. The furnace roared, the sparks flew, the engine picked up speed, but still their pursuers drew nearer. Sighing, the engine driver wiped his brow with his handkerchief and said, "I'm afraid it's no good, Toad. You see, they have a light load, and a better engine. You have only one chance, so listen very carefully to me. A short way ahead of us is a long tunnel, and on the other side of that is a thick woods. I will go through the tunnel as fast as I can, but the other fellows will naturally slow down a bit, for fear of an accident. When we are through the tunnel, I will hit the brakes as hard as I can. As soon as I do that, you must jump and hide in the woods before they get through the tunnel and see you. Then I will go full speed ahead again, and they can chase me as far as they like. Now get ready to jump when I tell you!"

They piled on more coals, the train shot

into the tunnel, and the engine rushed and roared and rattled, until at last they shot out the other end into fresh air and the peaceful moonlight and saw the woods lying dark on either side. The driver put on the brakes, the Toad got down on the step, and as the train slowed down to almost a walking pace he heard the driver call out, “Now, jump!”

Toad jumped, rolled down a short embankment, picked himself up unhurt, scrambled into the wood and hid.

Peeping out, he saw his train pick up speed again and disappear at a great pace. Then out of the tunnel burst the pursuing engine, roaring and whistling. Her crew was waving their weapons and shouting, “Stop! stop! stop!” When they were gone, the Toad had a hearty laugh—for the first time since he was thrown into prison.

But he soon stopped laughing when he began to think that it was now very late and dark and cold, and he was in an unknown woods, with no money and no chance of supper, and still far from friends and home. The dead silence of everything, after the roar and rattle of the train, was shocking. He did not dare leave the shelter of the trees, so he headed into the woods, thinking he should get as far away from the train track as possible.

After so many weeks within walls, he found the woods strange and unfriendly. The noise of the night birds sounded like searchers closing in on him. An owl, swooping silently toward him, brushed his shoulder with its wing, making him jump. Once he met a fox who stopped and said, "Hey, washerwoman! I was missing a pair of socks and a pillowcase this week! Don't let it happen again!" and trotted off snickering. Toad looked for a stone to throw at him, but could not succeed in finding one, which irritated him. At last, cold, hungry, and tired out, he lay down under a hollow tree. With branches and dead leaves he made himself as comfortable a bed as he could, and slept soundly till the morning.

CHAPTER 9

The Further Adventures of Toad

The front door of the hollow tree faced eastward, so the rising sun woke Toad at an early hour. The extreme coldness of his toes also helped rouse him. He had been dreaming that he was at home in bed in his own handsome room on a cold winter's night, and that his blankets had gotten up, grumbling that they couldn't stand the cold any longer, and had run downstairs to the kitchen fire to warm themselves.

Sitting up, he rubbed his eyes first and his half-frozen toes next. He wondered for a moment where he was, and looked around for his prison cell's familiar stone wall and little barred window. Then, with a leap of the heart, he remembered everything—he was free!

Free! The word alone was worth fifty warm blankets. He shook himself and combed the dry leaves out of his hair with his fingers, then marched forth into the morning sun. He felt cold but confident, hungry but hopeful. All his nervous terrors of yesterday had been chased away by rest and sleep and sunshine.

He had the world all to himself, that early summer morning. This was all very well ordinarily, but Toad was looking for someone who could tell him which way he ought to go. Soon he found himself walking along a quiet country road, which itself ran alongside a canal. Toad's spirits lifted still more because, as he told himself, "This road and canal must come FROM somewhere, and be going TO somewhere else. This is progress!" So he marched on patiently by the water's edge.

Round a bend in the road came plodding a horse. A rope tied to its collar stretched into the canal and attached to a barge, and aboard the barge was a big stout woman wearing a linen sunbonnet.

"A nice morning, ma'am!" she remarked to Toad as she drew near him.

"It is indeed!" responded Toad politely, as he walked along the towpath alongside her. "I dare it IS a nice morning for people who aren't in great trouble like I am. You see, my married daughter sent me a message to come to her at once. So off I went, not knowing what the trouble is but fearing the worst, as you will understand, ma'am, if you're a mother, too. And I've left my business to look after itself—I'm a washerwoman, you see. Worse yet, I've left my young children to look after *themselves*, and a more mischievous set of young imps doesn't exist, ma'am. To top it off I've lost all my money, and lost my way, and I hate to think what may be happening to my poor married daughter!"

"Where does your married daughter live, ma'am?" asked the bargewoman.

"She lives near to the river, ma'am," replied Toad. "Close to a fine house called Toad Hall, that's somewhere in these parts. Perhaps you have heard of it."

"Toad Hall? Why, I'm going that way myself," replied the bargewoman. "This canal joins the river some miles further on, a little above Toad Hall, and then it's an easy walk. I'll give you a lift."

She steered the barge close to the bank, and Toad, with many thanks, stepped on board and sat down. "Toad's luck again!" he thought. "I always come out on top!"

"So you're in the washing business,

ma'am?" said the bargewoman politely, as they glided along. "That must be a very fine business to be in."

"Finest business in the whole country," said Toad airily. "All the rich gentlemen come to me—they wouldn't go to anyone else. You see, I understand my work thoroughly. Washing, ironing, starching—I see to it all."

"But surely you don't DO all that work yourself, ma'am?" asked the bargewoman respectfully.

"Oh, I have employees," said Toad lightly: "twenty or thereabouts, always at work. But you know how employees are, ma'am! I must keep after 'em every minute!"

"I certainly do!" said the bargewoman heartily. "But I dare say you know how to handle yours, the lazy things! And are you very fond of washing?"

"I love it," said Toad. "I simply dote on it. I'm never so happy as when I've got both arms in the washtub."

"What a bit of luck, meeting you!" observed the bargewoman, thoughtfully. "A piece of good fortune for both of us!"

"Why, what do you mean?" asked Toad, nervously.

"Well, look at me, now," replied the bargewoman. "I like washing, just as you do.

But my husband is such a fellow for dodging work and leaving the barge to me, I get no time for that sort of thing. He ought to be here right now, either steering or caring for the horse. Instead, he's gone off with the dog, to see if they can't get a rabbit for dinner. He says he'll catch up with me further down the canal. But who knows if that will happen? I don't trust him once he gets off with that dog, who's worse than he is. But meantime, how am I to do my washing?"

"Oh, never mind about the washing," said Toad, not liking this subject at all. "Try and think about that rabbit for supper. I'm sure he'll find a nice fat young one. Got any onions?"

"I can't think about anything but my washing," said the bargewoman, "and I wonder how you can talk about rabbits, with such a joyful prospect in front of you. There's a heap of dirty clothes in a corner of the cabin. If you'll just take them and put them through the washtub as we go along, why, it'll be a pleasure for you and a real help to me. You'll find a tub handy, and soap, and a kettle on the stove, and a bucket to haul up water from the canal. Then I'll know you're enjoying yourself, instead of sitting here bored."

"Here, you let me steer!" said Toad, now

thoroughly frightened, "and then you can get on with your washing your own way. I might spoil your things, or not do 'em as you like. I'm more used to gentlemen's things myself."

"Let you steer?" replied the bargewoman, laughing. "It takes some practice to steer a barge properly. Besides, it's dull work, and I want you to be happy. No, you shall do the washing you are so fond of, and I'll stick to the steering that I understand. Don't deny me the pleasure of giving you a treat!"

Toad was cornered. He looked in vain for an escape, then sullenly gave in. "Well," he said to himself, "I suppose any fool can WASH!"

He fetched the tub, soap, and other necessities from the cabin, selected a few garments, tried to remember anything he had seen in casual glances through laundry windows, and went to work.

A long half-hour passed, and with every minute Toad grew crosser. Nothing that he could do seemed to do any good. Once or twice he looked nervously over his shoulder at the bargewoman, but she appeared to be absorbed in her steering. His back ached badly, and he noticed with dismay that his paws were beginning to get all crinkly. He muttered under his breath words that should never pass the lips of either washerwomen or Toads. Then he lost the soap for the fiftieth time.

A burst of laughter made him straighten himself and look round. The bargewoman was leaning back and laughing until the tears ran down her cheeks.

"I've been watching you all the time," she gasped. "I thought you must be a phony all along, from the conceited way you talked. Some washerwoman you are! Never washed so much as a dishcloth in your life, I'll bet!"

Toad's temper which had been simmering for some time, now boiled over. He lost all control of himself.

"You common, low, FAT bargewoman!" he shouted; "don't you dare talk to your superiors like that! Washerwoman indeed! I'll have you know that I am a Toad, a very well-known, respected, distinguished Toad! I may be in difficult circumstances just now, but I will NOT be laughed at by a bargewoman!"

The woman moved nearer and peered under his bonnet. "Why, so you are!" she cried. "A horrid, nasty, crawly Toad! And in my nice clean barge, too! Now that is a thing that I will NOT have."

She let go of the tiller for a moment. One big brawny arm shot out and caught Toad by a front leg, while the other grabbed him by a hind leg. Then the world turned suddenly upside down as Toad found himself flying through the air, revolving rapidly as he went.

The water, when he eventually reached it with a loud splash, was very chilly, but not cold enough to cool his furious temper. He rose to the surface spluttering. When he had wiped the duckweed out of his eyes, the first thing he saw was the bargewoman looking back at him over the stern of the retreating barge and laughing. He swore, as he coughed and choked, to get even with her.

He swam for the shore, his dress slowing him down greatly. When he finally touched land he found it hard to climb up the steep bank. Then, picking up his wet skirt, he started to run after the barge as fast as his legs would carry him, thirsting for revenge.

The bargewoman was still laughing when he drew up level with her. "Give your face a good wash, washerwoman," she called, "and iron it well, and you'll pass for quite a decent-looking Toad!"

Toad never paused to reply. Solid revenge was what he wanted, not some cheap verbal triumph (though he had a thing or two in his mind that he would have liked to say). He saw what he wanted ahead of him. He caught up

with the horse, unfastened the towrope and threw it aside, jumped lightly on the horse's back, and urged it to a gallop by kicking it vigorously in the sides. Leaving the towpath, he headed for open country. He looked back to see that the barge had run aground on the other side of the canal, and the bargewoman was waving wildly and shouting, "Stop, stop, stop!"

"I've heard that song before," said Toad, laughing, as he galloped on.

The barge horse was not capable of moving very fast for very long, and its gallop soon slowed to an easy walk. But Toad was quite content to know that he was moving, and the barge was not. He traveled on happily, growing drowsy in the hot sunshine. The horse eventually stopped, lowered his head, and began to nibble the grass. Toad, waking up, looked about him and found he was in a wide meadow. Near him stood a gypsy caravan, and beside it a man was sitting on a bucket turned upside down, very busy smoking and staring into the wide world. A fire burned nearby, and over the fire hung an iron pot, and out of that pot came forth quite delicious smells, which reminded Toad how very hungry he really was. He looked at the Gypsy; the Gypsy sat and smoked, and looked at him.

Presently the Gypsy took his pipe out of his mouth and remarked in a careless way, "Want to sell that horse of yours?"

Toad was very surprised. But then he remembered that Gypsies were very fond of horse-dealing, and that caravans needed horses to pull them. It had not occurred to him to turn the horse into cash, but the Gypsy's suggestion seemed to provide two good things: money, and a solid breakfast.

"What?" he said, "Sell this beautiful young horse of mine? Oh, no; it's out of the question. Who's going to take the washing to my customers every week? Besides, I'm too fond of him."

"Try and love a donkey," suggested the Gypsy. "Some people do."

"You don't seem to see," continued Toad, "that this fine horse of mine is something very special. He's a thoroughbred, partly; not the part you see, of course—another part. No, I simply couldn't think of selling him. All the same, how much might you offer for this beautiful young horse of mine?"

The Gypsy looked the horse over, and then he looked Toad over with equal care, and looked at the horse again. "A dollar a leg," he said briefly, and turned away, continuing to smoke and stare.

"A dollar a leg?" cried Toad. "I must work that out, and see what it comes to."

He climbed down off his horse, and sat by the Gypsy, and counted on his fingers. At last he said, "Why, that comes to only four dollars! Oh, no; I could not think of accepting four dollars for this beautiful young horse of mine."

"Well," said the Gypsy, "I'll tell you what I'll do. I'll make it five dollars, and that's seventy-five cents more than the animal's worth. And that's my last word."

Then Toad sat and thought long and deeply. For he was hungry and penniless, and still some distance from home, and enemies might still be looking for him. To someone in such a situation, five dollars appeared a good sum of money. On the other hand, it did not seem enough to get for a horse. But then, again, the horse hadn't cost *him* anything, so whatever he got was profit.

At last he said firmly, "Look here, my good man! I'll tell you what we will do, and this is MY last word. You shall give me six and a half dollars. In addition, you shall give me as much breakfast as I can eat out of that iron pot of yours that is sending forth such delicious and exciting smells. In return, I will give you my spirited young horse, with all the beautiful harness thrown in. If that's not good enough for you, say so, and I'll be going on. I know a man near here who's wanted this horse of mine for years."

The Gypsy grumbled frightfully, and declared if he did a few more deals of that sort he'd be ruined. But in the end he lugged a canvas bag out of his trouser pocket, and counted out six and a half dollars into Toad's paw. Then he disappeared into the caravan for an instant, and returned with a large iron plate and a knife, fork, and spoon. He tilted up the pot, and a glorious stream of hot rich stew gurgled into the plate. It was, indeed, the most beautiful stew in the world, being made of partridges, and pheasants, and chickens, and rabbits, and one or two other things. Toad took the plate on his lap, almost crying with pleasure, and stuffed, and stuffed, and stuffed, and kept asking for more, and the Gypsy never grudged him a mouthful. He thought that he had never eaten so good a breakfast in all his life.

When Toad had eaten as much stew as he could possibly hold, he got up and said good-bye to the Gypsy, and gave an affectionate farewell to the horse. The Gypsy, who knew the riverside well, told him which way to go, and he set forth again in the best possible spirits.

He was, indeed, a very different Toad from an hour ago. The sun was shining brightly, his wet clothes were quite dry again, he had money in his pocket, and he was nearing home and friends and safety. Best of all, he had had a substantial meal, and felt big, and strong, and careless, and self-confident.

As he tramped along happily, he thought of his adventures and escapes, and how when things seemed at their worst he always managed to find a way out. His pride began to swell within him. "Ho, ho!" he said to himself as he marched along with his head held high. "What a clever Toad I am! There is surely no animal as clever as me in the whole world! My enemies shut me up in prison, watched night and day by guards. I walk out through them all. They pursue me with train engines, and policemen, and pistols. I snap my fingers at them, and vanish, laughing. I am, unfortunately, thrown into a canal by a very evil-minded woman. What of it? I swim ashore, I seize her horse, I ride off in triumph, and I sell the horse for a pocketful of money and an excellent breakfast! Ho, ho! I am the Toad, the handsome, the popular, the successful Toad!" He got so puffed up with conceit that he made up a song in praise of himself as he walked. It was perhaps the most conceited song that any animal ever composed.

The world has held great Heroes,
As history books have showed;
But never a name has gone down to fame
Compared with that of Toad!

The clever men at Oxford
Know all that there is to be knowed.
But none of them know half as much
As intelligent Mr. Toad!

The animals sat in the Ark and cried,
Their tears in torrents flowed.
Who was it said, "There's land ahead?"
Encouraging Mr. Toad!

The army all saluted
As they marched along the road.
Was it the King? Or Emperor? No.
It was Mr. Toad.

The Queen and her Ladies-in-waiting
Sat at the window and sewed.
She cried, "Look! Who's that
HANDSOME man?"
They answered, "Mr. Toad."

There was a great deal more of the same sort, but it is too dreadfully conceited to be written down. These are some of the milder verses.

He sang as he walked, and he walked as he sang, and got prouder every minute. But his pride was shortly to have a severe fall.

After some miles of country lanes he

reached the main road. As he turned into it, he saw a little speck in the distance. The speck turned into a dot and then into a blob, and then into something very familiar. Then a "poop-poop" of warning fell on his delighted ear.

"This is wonderful!" said the excited Toad. "This is real life again, this is the great world from which I have been missed so long! I will call to them, my brothers of the wheel, and tell them some sort of story, and they will give me a lift, perhaps, with luck, it may end in my driving up to Toad Hall in a motorcar! That will show old Badger!"

He stepped confidently out into the road to wave at the motorcar, which slowed down as it approached. But suddenly he became very pale. His heart turned to water, his knees shook under him, and he doubled up and collapsed with a sickening pain in his heart. And well he might, poor animal; for the approaching car was the same one he had stolen from the Red Lion Hotel on that fatal day when all his troubles began! And the people in it were the very same people he had sat and watched in the coffee room!

He sank down in a miserable heap in the road, murmuring to himself in despair, "It's all over now! Chains and policemen again! Prison again! Dry bread and water again! Oh, what a fool I have been! Why did I go strutting about the countryside, singing conceited songs, and hailing people in broad daylight, instead of hiding until dark and slipping home quietly by back ways! Oh, foolish Toad!"

The terrible motorcar drew slowly nearer and nearer, until at last he heard it stop in front of him. Two gentlemen got out and walked around the trembling heap of crumpled misery lying in the road. One of them said, "Oh dear! Here is a poor old thing who has fainted in the road! Perhaps she is overcome by the heat. Let us lift her into the car and take her to the village, where someone might know her."

They tenderly lifted Toad into the motorcar and propped him up with soft cushions, then drove on.

When Toad heard them talk in so kind a way, and knew that he was not recognized, he began to feel braver. He cautiously opened one eye.

"Look!" said one of the gentlemen, "she is better already. The fresh air is doing her good. How do you feel now, ma'am?"

"Thank you kindly, sir," said Toad in a feeble voice, "I'm feeling a great deal better!"

"Very good," said the gentleman. "Now keep still, and don't try to talk."

"I won't," said Toad. "I was only thinking, if I could sit on the front seat there, where I could get the fresh air in my face, I would soon be all right again."

"What a very sensible idea!" said the gentleman. "Of course you shall." So they carefully helped Toad into the front seat beside the driver, and on they went again.

Toad was almost crazed with excitement by now. He sat up, looked about him, and tried to beat down the old cravings that rose up and took possession of him.

"It is fate!" he said to himself. "Why resist?" He turned to the driver at his side.

"Please, sir," he said, "I wish you would let me try and drive the car for a little. I have been watching you carefully, and it looks so easy, and I would like to be able to tell my friends that I once drove a motorcar!"

The driver laughed heartily at the proposal, and answered with delight, "Bravo, ma'am! I like your spirit. Have a try. You won't do any harm."

Toad eagerly scrambled into the driver's seat, took the steering wheel in his hands, and pretended to listen to the instructions given to him. He started the car moving, very slowly at first.

The gentlemen clapped their hands, and

Toad heard them saying, "How well she does it! Imagine a washerwoman driving a car as well as that, the first time!"

Toad went a little faster; then faster still, and faster.

He heard the gentlemen call out warningly, "Be careful, ma'am!" And this annoyed him, and he began to lose his head.

The driver tried to interfere, but he pinned him down in his seat with one elbow, and stamped on the accelerator hard. The rush of air in his face, the hum of the engine, and the leap of the car beneath him intoxicated his weak brain. "Washerwoman, indeed!" he shouted recklessly. "Ho! ho! I am Toad, the motorcar thief, the prison escapee! Sit still, and you shall know what driving really is; for you are in the hands of the famous, the skillful, the fearless Toad!"

With a cry of horror everyone rose and flung themselves on him. "Grab him!" they cried, "seize the Toad, the wicked animal who stole our motorcar! Bind him, chain him, drag him to the police station! Down with the desperate and dangerous Toad!"

But alas—they should have remembered to stop the motorcar before trying anything of that sort. With a half-turn of the wheel Toad sent the car crashing through the low hedge that ran along the roadside. One mighty bound, and the wheels of the car were churning up the thick mud of a pond.

Toad found himself flying through the air, then landing with a thump in the soft rich grass of a meadow. Sitting up, he could just see the motorcar in the pond, nearly submerged. The gentlemen were floundering helplessly in the water.

He picked himself up rapidly, and began running as hard as he could. When he was able to think calmly, he began to giggle, and he laughed until he had to sit down under a hedge. "Ho, ho!" he cried out in self-admiration, "Toad again! Toad, as usual, comes out on the top! Who was it that got them to give him a lift? Who managed to get on the front seat for the sake of fresh air? Who persuaded them to let him drive? Who landed them all in a horse pond? Who escaped, leaving the narrow-minded, timid beasts in the mud where they should be? Why, Toad, of course; clever Toad, great Toad, GOOD Toad!"

Then he burst into song again, and chanted with uplifted voice—

The motorcar went Poop-poop-poop,
As it raced along the road.
Who was it that steered it into a pond?
Ingenious Mr. Toad!

"Oh, how clever I am! How clever, how clever, how very clev—"

A slight noise in the distance behind him made him turn his head and look. Oh horror! Oh misery! Oh despair!

Two fields away, a man in wet driving clothes and two large policemen were visible, running toward him as hard as they could go!

Poor Toad sprang to his feet and began running again, his heart in his mouth. "Oh, my!" he gasped, as he panted along, "what an ASS I am! What a CONCEITED ass! Shouting and singing songs again!"

He glanced back, and saw to his dismay that they were getting closer. He did his best, but he was a fat animal, and his legs were short. He could hear them close behind him now. Not looking where he was going, he struggled on blindly, glancing back over his shoulder at the enemy. Then suddenly the earth fell away under his feet and, splash! He found himself over his head in deep water, rapid water. In his panic he had run straight into the river!

He rose to the surface and tried to grasp the reeds that grew along the water's edge, but the current was so strong that it tore them out of his hands. "Oh my!" gasped poor Toad, "if I ever steal a motorcar again . . .

If ever I sing another conceited song"—then down he went, and came up breathless and spluttering. Presently he saw that he was approaching a big dark hole in the bank, just above his head. As the stream bore him past, he reached up and caught hold of the edge of the hole. Then slowly and with difficulty he pulled himself up out of the water, until he was able to rest his elbows on the edge of the hole. There he remained for some minutes, for he was quite exhausted.

As he panted and stared before him into the dark hole, something small and bright twinkled in its depths, moving toward him. As it approached, a face grew up gradually around it, and it was a familiar face!

Brown and small, with whiskers.

Grave and round, with neat ears and silky hair.

It was the Water Rat!

CHAPTER 10

Like Summer Tempests Came His Tears

The Rat put out a little brown paw, gripped Toad firmly by the scruff of the neck, and gave a great pull. The waterlogged Toad came up slowly but surely over the edge of the hole, until at last he stood safe and sound in the hall, streaked with mud and seaweed, and with water streaming off him. But he was happy and high-spirited as ever before, now that he found himself in the home of a friend.

"Oh, Ratty!" he cried. "I've been through so much since I saw you last, you can't imagine! Such trials, such sufferings, and I bore it all so nobly! Then such escapes, such disguises, such tricks, all so cleverly planned! I've been in prison—got out of it, of course! Been thrown into a canal—swam ashore! Stole a horse—sold him for a large sum of money! Tricked everybody—made 'em all do exactly what I wanted! Oh, I AM a smart Toad, and no mistake! What do you think my last adventure was? Just wait until I tell you—"

"Toad," said the Water Rat, very firmly, "you go off upstairs at once, and take off that dress, and clean yourself thoroughly, and put on some of my clothes, and try and come down looking like a gentleman if you CAN. I've never seen a more shabby, bedraggled object in my whole life! Now, stop swaggering and arguing, and go! I'll have something to say to you later."

At first, Toad was inclined to talk back to Rat. He had had enough of being ordered about when he was in prison. However, after he caught sight of himself in the hall mirror, with the filthy black bonnet hanging over one eye, he changed his mind and went very quickly upstairs. There he washed and brushed-up thoroughly and changed his clothes. Once he was dressed, he stood for a long time admiring himself in the mirror, thinking what idiots people were to ever have mistaken him for a washerwoman.

By the time he came down again, lunch was on the table. Toad was very glad to see it, for he had been through a lot since the excellent breakfast provided by the Gypsy. While they ate Toad told the Rat all his adventures, spending a great deal of time describing his own cleverness and cool-headedness in emergencies, and all in all suggesting that he had had a marvelous and highly enjoyable adventure. But the more he talked and boasted, the more grave and silent the Rat became.

Finally Toad had talked himself out. There was silence for a while, and then the Rat said, "Now, Toady, I don't want to hurt you, after all you've been through. But seriously, don't you see what an awful idiot you've made of yourself? You yourself admit that you've been handcuffed, imprisoned, starved, chased, terrified out of your life, insulted, jeered at, and shamefully flung into the water! Where's the fun in that? And all because you had to go and steal a motorcar. You know that from the first moment you set eyes on a motorcar, you've never had anything but trouble with them. But if you MUST be mixed up with them, why STEAL them? Cripple yourself in an accident, if you think that's exciting. Go bankrupt, if that makes you happy—but why choose to be a convict? When are you going to think of your friends, and try not to embarrass them? Do you suppose I enjoy going about, hearing animals say that I'm the chap who hangs about with jailbirds?"

Now, one of Toad's better points was that he was a truly good-hearted animal who never minded hearing straight talk from his real friends. It is true that while Rat was talking, he kept making rebellious remarks to himself, such as "But it WAS fun, though! Great fun!" But when the Rat had finished, he heaved a deep sigh and said, very nicely and humbly, "Quite right, Ratty! How sensible you always are! Yes, I've been a conceited old ass, I can see that now. As for motorcars, I've sort of lost interest in them since last ducking in that river of yours. The fact is, while I was hanging on to the edge of your hole and getting my breath, I had a really brilliant idea about motorboats—There, there, Ratty! Don't get so upset. It was only an idea, and we won't talk about it now. We'll have our coffee and a quiet chat, and then I'm going to stroll down to Toad Hall and get back to my old way of life. I've had enough of adventures. I shall lead a quiet, steady, respectable life, puttering about my property, and improving it, and doing a little landscape gardening. There will always be a good dinner for friends when they come to see me, and I will keep a pony-cart to travel about in, just as I used to in the good old days."

"Stroll down to Toad Hall?" cried the

Rat, greatly excited. "What are you talking about? Do you mean to say you haven't HEARD?"

"Heard what?" said Toad, turning rather pale. "Go on, Ratty! Quick! What haven't I heard?"

"Do you mean to tell me," shouted the Rat, thumping his little fist upon the table, "that you've heard nothing about the stoats and weasels?"

"No, not a word!" cried Toad, trembling in every limb. "What have they been doing?"

"They've taken Toad Hall!" announced the Rat.

Toad leaned his elbows on the table, and his chin on his paws. A large tear welled up in each of his eyes, overflowed and splashed on the table, plop! plop!

"Go on, Ratty," he murmured presently; "tell me all. The worst is over. I can bear it."

"When you got into that that trouble of yours," said the Rat slowly; "I mean, when you—disappeared from society for a time, over that misunderstanding about a—a machine, you know—"

Toad nodded.

"Well, everyone around here talked about it, naturally," continued the Rat, "not only along the riverside, but even in the Wild

Wood. Animals took sides, as always happens. The Riverbankers stuck up for you, and said you had been badly treated. But the Wild Wooders said harsh things. And they got very cocky, and went about saying you were done for, and that you would never come back again, ever!"

Toad nodded once more, still silent.

"That's the sort of nasty beasts they are," the Rat went on. "But Mole and Badger, they stuck up for you, through thick and thin, and kept saying that you would come back again soon. They didn't know exactly how, but somehow!"

Toad began to sit up in his chair again, and to smile a little.

"So they arranged to move their things in to Toad Hall, and sleep there, and keep it tidy, and have it all ready for you when you turned up. They didn't guess what was going to happen, of course; still, they had their suspicions about the Wild Wood animals. Now I come to the most painful and tragic part of my story. It was a very dark night, when it was blowing hard, too, and raining cats and dogs. A band of weasels, armed to the teeth, crept silently up to the front entrance. At the same time, a group of ferrets, coming through the kitchen garden, took over the backyard and offices.

And meanwhile, a company of stoats sneaked into the music room.

"The Mole and the Badger were sitting by the fire in the library, telling stories and suspecting nothing, when those bloodthirsty villains broke down the doors and rushed them from every side. They made the best fight they could, but what could they do? They were unarmed, and taken by surprise, and there were two of them against several hundred. The Wild Wooders beat them severely with sticks, those two poor faithful creatures, and threw them out into the cold and the wet, with many insulting remarks!

"And the Wild Wooders have been living in Toad Hall ever since," continued the Rat. "I'm told they lie in bed half the day, and eat at all hours, and the place is such a mess it's not fit to be seen! They're eating your grub, and drinking your drink, and making bad jokes about you, and singing vulgar songs, about—well, about prisons and judges, and policemen. And they're telling the merchants and everybody that they've come to stay forever."

"Oh, have they!" said Toad getting up and seizing a stick. "I'll soon see about that!"

"It's no good, Toad!" called the Rat after him. "You'd better come back and sit down; you'll only get into trouble."

But the Toad was off, and there was no stopping him. He marched rapidly down the road, his stick over his shoulder, fuming and muttering in anger. When he reached his front gate, out popped a long yellow ferret with a gun.

"Who goes there?" said the ferret sharply.

"Oh, come off it!" said Toad, very angrily. "What do you mean by speaking to me like that? Come out here at once, or I'll—"

The ferret said never a word, but he brought his gun up to his shoulder. Toad sensibly dropped flat in the road, and BANG! a bullet whistled over his head.

The startled Toad scrambled to his feet and ran off down the road as fast as he could. As he ran he heard the ferret laughing.

He went back, very downhearted, and told the Water Rat.

"What did I tell you?" said the Rat. "It's no good. They've got guards posted, and they are all armed. You must just wait."

Still, Toad did not want to give in all at once. So he got out the boat and rowed up the river to the front of Toad Hall.

Arriving within sight of his old home, he rested on his oars and surveyed the land cautiously. Everything seemed peaceful and quiet. He could see the whole front of Toad

Hall, glowing in the evening sunshine; the pigeons settling along the line of the roof; the garden, a blaze of flowers; the creek that led up to the boathouse, the little bridge that crossed it. All seemed to be waiting for his return. He would try the boathouse first, he thought. Very carefully he paddled up to the mouth of the creek, and was just passing under the bridge, when . . . CRASH!

A great stone smashed through the bottom of the boat, which filled and sank. Toad found himself struggling in deep water. Looking up, he saw two stoats leaning over the bridge and giggling wildly. "It will be your head next time, Toady!" they called out to him. The indignant Toad swam to shore, while the stoats laughed themselves nearly into fits.

The Toad made his weary way home on foot, and again told the Water Rat of his disappointing experience.

"Well, WHAT did I tell you?" said the Rat very crossly. "And now see what you've done! Lost my boat that I was so fond of! And ruined that nice suit of clothes that I lent you! Really, Toad, of all the annoying animals—I wonder how you manage to keep any friends at all!"

The Toad saw how foolishly he had acted. He apologized to Rat for losing his boat and spoiling his clothes. And he wound up by saying, "Ratty! I see that I have been a headstrong and a willful Toad! From now on, believe me, I will do nothing without your advice and full approval."

"If that is really so," said the good-natured Rat, "then my advice to you is to sit down and have your supper, and be very patient. For I am convinced that we can do nothing until we have seen the Mole and the Badger, and talked all this over and heard their advice."

"Ah, yes, of course, dear Mole and

Badger," said Toad, lightly. "What's become of them, anyway? I had forgotten all about them."

"Well you might ask!" said the Rat reproachfully. "While you were riding about the country in expensive motorcars, and galloping on thoroughbred horses, those two poor animals have been camping outside, in every sort of weather, keeping watch over your house and scheming how to get it back for you. You don't deserve to have such true and loyal friends, Toad, you really don't. Some day, when it's too late, you'll be sorry you didn't value them more while you had them!"

"I'm an ungrateful beast, I know," sobbed Toad, shedding bitter tears. "Let me go out and find them, out into the cold, dark night, and share their hardships, and try and prove that—Wait a minute! I hear the rattle of dishes on a tray! Supper's here at last, hooray! Come on, Ratty!"

The Rat reminded himself that poor Toad had been eating prison food for quite a long time, and that he needed to be forgiving. He followed him to the table, and urged him to eat heartily.

They had just finished their meal when there came a heavy knock at the door.

Toad was nervous, but the Rat, nodding

mysteriously at him, went straight to the door and opened it. In walked Mr. Badger.

It was clear from his appearance that he had been away from the comforts of home for some time. His shoes were covered with mud, and he was looking very rough and tousled. He came solemnly up to Toad, shook him by the paw, and said, "Welcome home, Toad! Alas, what am I saying? Home, indeed! This is a poor homecoming. Unhappy Toad!" Then he turned his back on him, sat down to the table, and helped himself to a large slice of cold pie.

Toad was alarmed at this very serious style of greeting. But the Rat whispered to him, "Never mind; he's always rather downhearted when he's hungry. In half an hour he'll be quite different."

So they waited in silence, and presently there came another, lighter knock. The Rat went to the door and brought in the Mole, very shabby and unwashed, with bits of hay and straw sticking in his fur.

"Hooray! Here's old Toad!" cried the Mole, his face beaming. "It's so good to have you back again!" And he began to dance around him. "We never dreamed you would turn up so soon! Why, you must have escaped, you clever Toad!"

Very alarmed, the Rat nudged the Mole sharply, but it was too late. Toad was puffing and swelling already.

"Clever? Oh, no!" he said. "I'm not really clever, according to my friends. I've only broken out of the strongest prison in England, that's all! And captured a railway train and escaped on it, that's all! And disguised myself and gone about the country fooling everybody, that's all! Oh, no! I'm a stupid old Toad, I am! I'll tell you one or two of my little adventures, Mole, and you shall judge for yourself!"

"Well, well," said the Mole, moving toward the supper table; "suppose you talk while I eat. I haven't had a bite since breakfast!" And he sat down and helped himself to cold beef and pickles.

Toad settled himself on the rug, thrust his paw into his trouser pocket, and pulled out a handful of silver. "Look at that!" he cried, displaying it. "That's not so bad, is it, for a few minutes' work? And how do you think I did it, Mole? Horse-dealing! That's how I did it!"

"Go on, Toad," said the Mole, immensely interested.

"Toad, do be quiet, please!" said the Rat. "And don't encourage him, Mole. Tell us what the situation is, and what we should do, now that Toad is back."

"The situation is about as bad as it can be," replied the Mole. "And as for what's to be done, I'm blessed if I know! The Badger and I have been round and round the place, by night and by day. It's always the same thing. Guards posted everywhere, guns poked out at us, stones thrown at us. There's always someone on the lookout, and when they see us, how they laugh! That's what annoys me most!"

"It's a very difficult situation," said the Rat. "But I think I see now what Toad really ought to do. He ought to—"

"No, he shouldn't!" shouted the Mole, with his mouth full. "Nothing of the sort! You don't understand. What he ought to do is, he ought to—"

"Well, I won't do it, anyway!" cried Toad, getting excited. "I'm not going to be ordered about by you fellows! It's my house we're talking about, and I know exactly what to do, and I'll tell you. I'm going to—"

By this time they were all talking at once, at the top of their voices, and the noise was simply deafening. Then a thin, dry voice said, "Be quiet, all of you!" and instantly everyone was silent.

It was the Badger, who had finished his

pie and was looking at them severely. When he saw that he had gotten their attention, he turned back to the table again and reached for the cheese. And so great was their respect for that animal that not another word was spoken until he had finished his meal and brushed the crumbs from his knees. The Toad fidgeted a good deal, but the Rat held him firmly down.

When the Badger was ready, he got up from his seat and stood before the fireplace, thinking deeply. At last he spoke.

"Toad!" he said severely. "You bad, troublesome little animal! Aren't you ashamed of yourself? What do you think your father, my old friend, would say if he had been here tonight, and knew of all your goings on?"

Toad, who was on the sofa by this time, rolled over on his face and sobbed.

"There, there!" went on the Badger, more kindly. "Never mind. Stop crying. We're going to let bygones be bygones, and try and turn over a new leaf. But what the Mole says is quite true. The stoats are on guard at every point, and they make the best lookouts in the world. It's quite useless to think of attacking the place. They're too strong for us."

"Then it's all over," sobbed the Toad, crying into the sofa cushions. "I will go and join the army, and never see my dear Toad

Hall any more!"

"Come, cheer up, Toady!" said the Badger. "There are more ways of getting a place back than taking it by storm. I haven't said my last word yet. Now I'm going to tell you a great secret."

Toad sat up slowly and dried his eyes. Secrets had an immense attraction for him. This was mostly because he never could keep one, and he enjoyed a sort of unholy thrill when he went and told another animal, after having faithfully promised not to.

"There is an underground passage," said the Badger, impressively, "that leads from the riverbank, quite near here, right up into the middle of Toad Hall."

"Oh, nonsense, Badger," said Toad. "You've been listening to the yarns they spin in the pubs around here. I know every inch of Toad Hall, inside and out. There's nothing of the sort, I promise you!"

"My young friend," said the Badger, very severely, "your father, who was a worthy animal—a lot worthier than some I know—was a great friend of mine. He told me many things he wouldn't have dreamed of telling you. He discovered that passage. He didn't create it, of course; that was done hundreds of years before. But he repaired it and cleaned it out, because he thought it might come in useful some day. 'Don't let my son know about it,' he said. 'He's a good boy, but rather silly, and he simply cannot hold his tongue. If he's ever in a real fix, and it would be of use to him, you may tell him about the secret passage, but not before.'"

The other animals looked hard at Toad to see how he would take this bit of news. He looked a bit sulky at first, but then he brightened up, like the good fellow he was.

"Well, well," he said, "perhaps I am a bit of a talker. I'm a popular fellow, and when my friends and I get together—well, we joke, we sparkle, we tell witty stories, and sometimes my tongue gets wagging. I have the gift of conversation. Go on, Badger. How's this passage of yours going to help us?"

"I've found out a thing or two lately," continued the Badger. "I got Otter to disguise himself as a chimney-sweep and stop at Toad Hall with brushes over his shoulder, asking for a job. There's going to be a big banquet tomorrow night. It's somebody's birthday—the Chief Weasel's, I believe—and all the weasels will be gathered together in the dining hall. They'll be eating and drinking and laughing and carrying on, suspecting nothing. No guns, no swords, no sticks, no weapons whatever!"

"But the lookouts will be posted as usual," remarked the Rat.

"Exactly," said the Badger; "that is my point. The weasels will depend entirely on their excellent lookouts. And that is where the passage comes in. That very useful tunnel leads right up into the butler's pantry, next to the dining hall!"

"Aha! that squeaky board in the butler's pantry!" said Toad. "Now I understand it!"

"We shall creep out quietly into the butler's pantry—" cried the Mole.

"—with our pistols and swords and sticks—" shouted the Rat.

"—and rush in upon them," said the Badger.

"—and whack 'em, and whack 'em, and whack 'em!" cried the Toad joyously, running round and round the room, and jumping over the chairs.

"Very well, then," said the Badger, "our plan is settled. So, as it's getting very late, all of you go right off to bed. We will make all the necessary arrangements in the morning."

Toad went off to bed—he knew better than to argue—although he was feeling too excited to sleep. But he had had a long day, and sheets and blankets felt awfully nice compared to straw spread on the stone floor of a drafty cell. His head had not been on his pillow for many seconds before he was snoring happily.

He slept late the next morning, and by the time he came downstairs the other animals had finished their breakfast. The Mole had gone off somewhere by himself. The Badger sat in the armchair, reading the paper, not at all concerned about what was going to happen that evening. The Rat, on the other hand, was running round the room busily, his arms full of weapons of every kind. He was making four little heaps on the floor, muttering under his breath, "Here's-a-sword-for-the-Rat, here's-a-sword-for-the-Mole, here's-a-sword-for-the-Toad, here's-a-sword-for-the-Badger! Here's-a-pistol-for-the-Rat, here's-a-pistol-for-the-Mole, here's-a-pistol-for-the-Toad, here's-a-pistol-for-the-Badger!" And so on, while the four little heaps gradually grew and grew.

"That's fine, Rat," said the Badger presently, looking at the busy little animal over the edge of his newspaper. "I'm not stopping you. But once we get past the stoats, with those guns of theirs, we won't need any swords or pistols. Once we're inside the dining hall with our sticks, we'll clear out the lot of them in five minutes. I would do the whole thing by myself, only I don't want to deprive you fellows of the fun!"

"It's good to be on the safe side," said the Rat, polishing a pistol-barrel on his sleeve.

The Toad, having finished his breakfast, picked up a stout stick and swung it vigorously, beating imaginary animals. "I'll learn 'em to steal my house!" he cried. "I'll learn 'em, I'll learn 'em!"

"Don't say 'learn 'em,' Toad," said the Rat, greatly shocked. "It's not good English."

"What are you nagging at Toad for?" inquired the Badger. "What's the matter with his English? It's the same what I use myself, and if it's good enough for me, it ought to be good enough for you!"

"I'm very sorry," said the Rat humbly. "Only I THINK it ought to be 'teach 'em,' not 'learn 'em.' "

"But we don't WANT to teach 'em," replied the Badger. "We want to LEARN 'em—learn 'em, learn 'em! And what's more, we're going to DO it, too!"

"Oh, very well, have it your way," said the Rat. He was getting rather muddled about which was right himself.

Presently the Mole came into the room, obviously very pleased with himself. "I've been having such fun!" he announced. "I've been getting a rise out of the stoats!"

"I hope you've been very careful, Mole?" said the Rat anxiously.

"I should hope so, too," said the Mole confidently. "I got the idea when I found that old washerwoman dress that Toad came home in yesterday, hanging before the fire. So I put it on, and the bonnet and shawl as well, and off I went to Toad Hall, as bold as you please. The sentries were on the lookout, of course, with their guns and all the rest of their nonsense. 'Good morning, gentlemen!' says I, very respectful. 'Want any washing done today?'

"They looked at me very proud and stiff and haughty, and said, 'Go away, washerwoman! We don't do any washing on duty.' I said, 'Or any other time?' Ha, ha! Wasn't I funny, Toad?"

"Poor, silly animal!" said Toad, sounding very superior. The fact is, he felt very jealous of Mole for what he had just done. It was exactly what he would have liked to have done himself, if only he had thought of it first, and hadn't overslept.

"So the sergeant in charge, he said to me, 'Now run away, my good woman! Don't keep my men idling and talking on their posts.' 'Run away?' says I; 'it won't be me that'll be running away, a very short time from now!'"

"O MOLY, how could you?" said the Rat, dismayed.

The Badger laid down his paper.

"I could see them pricking up their ears and looking at each other," went on the Mole; "and the sergeant said to them, 'Never mind HER; she doesn't know what she's talking about.'"

"'Oh, don't I?' said I. 'Well, let me tell you this. My daughter washes for Mr. Badger, and that's how I know what I know! A hundred bloodthirsty badgers, armed with rifles, are going to attack Toad Hall this very night, coming through the meadow. Six boatloads of Rats, with pistols and swords, will come up the river and land in the garden. A select troop known as the Death-or-Glory Toads will storm the orchard. There won't be much left of you to wash by the time they're done with you, unless you clear out while you have the chance!' Then I ran away, but soon I came creeping back along the ditch and watched through the hedge. They were all as nervous and flustered as could be, running everywhere at once, and falling over each other, and everyone giving orders to everybody else and not listening. And I heard the stoats saying to each other, 'Isn't that just like the weasels? They'll sit comfortably in the banquet hall, having feasts and toasts and songs and all sorts of fun, while we must stand guard in the cold and dark, and end up cut to pieces by blood-thirsty Badgers!'"

"Oh, you idiot, Mole!" cried Toad. "You've spoiled everything!"

"Mole," said the Badger, in his dry, quiet way, "I see that you have more sense in your little finger than some other animals have in their entire fat bodies. You have done extremely well. Good Mole! Clever Mole!"

The Toad was simply wild with jealousy, especially because he couldn't begin to understand what the Mole had done that was so particularly clever. Fortunately for him, before he could lose his temper and expose himself to the Badger's sarcasm, the bell rang for lunch.

It was a simple but hearty meal, and when they were done, the Badger stretched out in the armchair and said, "Well, we've got our work cut out for us tonight, and it will probably be pretty late before we're through. I'm just going to take forty winks while I can." And he drew a handkerchief over his face and was soon snoring.

The anxious Rat resumed his preparations, and started running between his four little heaps, muttering, "Here's-a-belt-for-the-Rat, here's-a-belt-for-the-Mole, here's-a-belt-for-the-Toad, here's-a-belt-for-the-Badger!" and so on. Kindly Mole took Toad's arm, led him outside, shoved him into a lawn chair, and invited him to tell him all his adventures from beginning to end. This Toad was only too willing to do. The Mole was a good listener, and Toad rather let himself go. In fact, much of what he told Mole belonged in the what-might-have-happened-if-I-only-thought-of-it-in-time category instead of what-actually-happened. But those are always the best stories, and why shouldn't we enjoy telling them, instead of the rather ordinary things that really occur?

CHAPTER 11

The Return of the Hero

When it began to grow dark, the Rat, looking excited and mysterious, called them back into the parlor. He placed each animal alongside his little heap, then dressed them for the coming adventure. This took quite a long time. First, there was a belt to go round each animal, and then a sword to be stuck into each belt, and a dagger on the other side to balance it. Next came a pair of pistols, a policeman's nightstick, several sets of handcuffs, some bandages, and a drinking flask and sandwich case. The Badger laughed good-humoredly and said, "All right, Ratty! This entertains you, and it doesn't hurt me. But all I need is this here stick." But the Rat only said, "PLEASE, Badger. You know I wouldn't want you to blame me afterward and say I had forgotten ANYTHING!"

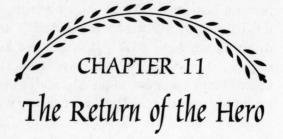

When everything was ready, the Badger took a lantern in one paw and grasped his great stick with the other. "Now then, follow me!" he said. "Mole goes first, 'cause I'm very pleased with him; Rat next; Toad last. And look here, Toady! Don't chatter as much as usual, or I'll send you back. See if I don't!"

The Toad was so anxious not to be left out that he accepted his lowly position without a murmur, and the animals set off. The Badger led them along by the river for a little way, and then suddenly swung over the edge into a hole in the riverbank, a little above the water. The Mole and the Rat followed silently, swinging themselves successfully into the hole as they had seen the Badger do. But when it was Toad's turn, he managed to slip and fall into the water with a loud splash and a squeal of alarm. He was hauled out by his friends, but the Badger was seriously angry. He told him that the very next time he made a fool of himself he would most certainly be left behind.

So at last they were in the secret passage, and the expedition had really begun!

It was cold, and dark, and damp, and narrow, and poor Toad began to shiver, partly from dread, and partly because he was so very wet. The lantern was far ahead, and he lagged behind a little in the darkness. Then he heard the Rat call out warningly, "COME on, Toad!" Terrified of being left behind in the darkness, he "came on" with such a rush that he bumped into the Rat, and the Rat knocked into the Mole and the Mole into the Badger, and for a moment all was confusion. The Badger thought they were being attacked from behind, and very nearly shot Toad. When he found out what had really happened he was very angry indeed, and said, "That's enough! Toad stays behind!"

But Toad whimpered, and the other two promised that they would make sure he behaved well. The group moved on, only this time the Rat was last, keeping a firm grip on Toad's shoulder.

So they groped and shuffled along, with their ears pricked up and their paws on their pistols, until at last the Badger said, "By now we ought to be pretty nearly under the Hall."

Then suddenly they heard, not far over their heads, a murmur of sounds. It was as if people were shouting and cheering and stamping and hammering on tables. The Toad felt more nervous than ever, but the Badger only remarked calmly, "The Weasels are going at it, aren't they?"

The passage now began to slope upward.

They groped on a little further, and then the noise grew more distinct with every second. "Hooray, hooray, hooray!" they heard, and the stamping of little feet on the floor, and the clinking of glasses "WHAT a time they're having!" said the Badger. "Come on!" They hurried along the passage until it ended, and they found themselves standing under a trapdoor that led up into the butler's pantry.

Such a tremendous noise was going on in the banquet hall that there was no danger of them being overheard. The Badger said, "Now, boys, all together!" and the four of them put their shoulders to the trapdoor and pushed with all their might until it opened. Then they scrambled into the pantry, with only a door between them and their unsuspecting enemies.

The noise was simply deafening. At last, as the cheering and hammering died away, a voice could be heard saying, "Well, I will not keep you much longer. But before I resume my seat, I would like to say one word about our kind host, Mr. Toad." There was a roar of laughter. "We all know Toad" (more laughter)—"GOOD Toad; MODEST Toad; HONEST Toad . . ." Howls of laughter were mixed with much cheering and shouts of glee.

"Just let me at him!" muttered Toad, grinding his teeth.

"Hold on a minute!" said the Badger, restraining Toad with difficulty. "Get ready, all of you!"

"—Let me sing you a little song," went on the voice, "which I have composed about our friend Mr. Toad"—(prolonged applause).

Then the Chief Weasel—for it was he—began to sing in a high, squeaky voice—

Toad he went a-wandering
Happily down the street—

The Badger took a firm grip of his stick with both paws, glanced around at his comrades, and cried—

"The hour is come! Follow me!"

He flung the door open wide.

And oh my!

What a squealing and a squeaking and a screeching filled the air!

The terrified weasels dived under the tables and sprang madly out the windows. Ferrets rushed wildly for the fireplace and got hopelessly jammed in the chimney. Tables and chairs were upset, and glass and china went crashing on the floor, in the panic of the terrible moment when the four Heroes strode furiously into the room! There was the mighty Badger, his whiskers bristling, his great staff whistling through the air. Mole, black and grim, waved his stick and shouted his awful war cry, "A Mole! A Mole!" Rat was an absolute desperado, his belt bulging with weapons of every variety. Toad, in a frenzy of excitement and injured pride, was swollen to twice his ordinary size. He leaped into the air, letting out Toad-whoops that chilled them to the bone as he headed straight for the Chief Weasel. They were only four in all, but to the panic-stricken weasels the hall seemed full of monstrous animals, whooping and waving enormous clubs. They fled with squeals of terror, this way and that, through the windows, up the chimney, anywhere to get out of reach of those terrible sticks.

The affair was soon over. Up and down

the whole length of the hall strode the four Friends, whacking sticks at every head that showed itself. In five minutes the room was cleared. Through the broken windows they could hear the shrieks of terrified weasels escaping across the lawn. On the floor lay a dozen or so of the enemy, whom the Mole was busy handcuffing. The Badger, resting from his labors, leaned on his stick and wiped his forehead.

"Mole," he said, "you're the best of fellows! Just glance outside and check on those sentries of yours, and see what they're doing. I believe that, thanks to you, we won't have much trouble with them tonight!"

The Mole vanished through a window, while the Badger instructed the other two to set a table on its legs again, pick up knives and forks and plates and glasses from the litter on the floor, and see if they could find anything for supper. "I want some grub, I do," he said. "Get a move on, Toad! We've got your house back for you, and you don't offer us so much as a sandwich." Toad felt rather hurt that the Badger didn't say pleasant things to him, and tell him how splendidly he had fought. He himself was rather pleased with the way he had gone for the Chief Weasel and sent him flying across the table with one blow of his stick. But he bustled about, and so did the Rat, and soon they found some jelly in a glass dish, and a cold chicken, some pudding, and quite a lot of lobster salad. In the pantry they came upon a basketful of rolls and plenty of cheese, butter, and celery. They were just about to sit down when the Mole climbed in through the window. He was chuckling, and carrying an armful of rifles.

"It's all over," he reported. "From what I can make out, as soon as the stoats heard the shrieks inside the hall, most of them threw down their rifles and ran. The others stayed for a bit, but when the weasels came rushing out the stoats thought the weasels had turned on them. They attacked the weasels, and the weasels fought to get away, and they wrestled and punched each other, and rolled over and over, until most of 'em rolled into the river. They've all disappeared by now, one way or another, and I've got their rifles."

"Excellent animal!" said the Badger, his mouth full of chicken and salad. "Now, there's just one more thing I want you to do, Mole, before you sit down to your supper. I'm sorry to trouble you, only I know I can trust you to get a thing done, and I wish I could say the same of everyone. I'd send Rat, if he wasn't a poet. I want you to take those fellows on the floor there upstairs, and make them clean the bedrooms. See that they sweep UNDER the beds, and put clean sheets and pillowcases on, and turn down one corner of the bedclothes, and have a pitcher of hot water, and clean towels, and fresh cakes of soap, put in each room. And then you can give them each a beating, if you like, and kick them out the back door. Then come along and have some of this roast chicken. It's first-rate. I'm very pleased with you, Mole!"

The good-natured Mole picked up a stick, formed his prisoners in a line and marched them upstairs. He returned after a bit, smiling, and said that every room was clean as a new pin. "And I didn't have to beat them, either," he added. "I thought, on the whole, they had had enough beating for one night. They were very respectful, and said they were extremely sorry for what they had done. They blamed it all on the Chief Weasel and the stoats, and said if they could ever do anything for us, we only have to ask. So I gave them each a roll, and let them out the back, and off they ran as hard as they could!"

Then the Mole pulled his chair up to the table, and pitched into the supper. Toad, like the gentleman he was, put his jealousy aside and said heartily, "Thank you, dear Mole, for all your work and trouble tonight, and especially for your cleverness this morning!" The Badger was pleased at that, and said, "There speaks a brave Toad!" So they finished their supper in great joy and contentment, and then enjoyed a well-earned rest between clean sheets. They were safe in Toad's ancestral home, won back by matchless courage, marvelous strategy, and a proper handling of sticks.

The following morning, Toad, who had overslept as usual, came down to breakfast disgracefully late. He found on the table a quantity of eggshells, some fragments of cold and leathery toast, a nearly empty coffeepot, and very little else. This did not improve his temper, considering that, after all, it was his own house. Through the windows of the breakfast room he could see the Mole and the Water Rat sitting in chairs out on the lawn, evidently telling each other stories. They were roaring with laughter and kicking their legs up in the air. The Badger, who was deep in the morning paper, merely nodded when Toad entered the room. But Toad knew better than to complain to Badger, so he sat down and made the best breakfast he could. He merely promised himself that he would get even with them all sooner or later.

When he had nearly finished, the Badger looked up and remarked, "I'm sorry, Toad, but I'm afraid there's a heavy morning's work in front of you. You see, we really ought to have a banquet at once, to celebrate this affair. It's expected of you—in fact, it's the rule. The invitations have to be written and sent off at once, and you've got to write 'em. Now, sit down at that table—there's stacks of letter-paper on it, with 'Toad Hall' at the top in blue and gold—and write invitations to all our friends. If you stick to it we shall get them out before lunch. I'll do my part, as well. I'll order the banquet."

"What!" cried Toad, dismayed. "Why should I stay indoors and write a lot of rotten letters on a morning like this, when I want to enjoy myself! Certainly not! I'd rather—But stop!" Toad's face quickly rearranged itself to look modestly pleased. "Why, of course, dear Badger! After all, my pleasure is nothing compared with that of others! If you wish it done, it shall be done. Go, Badger, order the banquet, order what you like. Then join our young Friends outside enjoying themselves, ignoring me and my cares and work. I am happy to sacrifice this fair morning on the altar of friendship!"

The Badger looked at him very suspiciously,

but Toad's honest face persuaded him that all was well. He left the room and headed toward the kitchen. Instantly, Toad hurried to the writing-table. A fine idea had occurred to him while he was talking. He WOULD write the invitations. He would be sure to mention the heroic part he had taken in the fight, and how he had laid the Chief Weasel flat. He would hint at his adventures, and what triumphant stories he had to tell. He would include a sort of program of entertainment for the evening— something like this, as he sketched it out in his head:

SPEECH . . . BY TOAD.

(There will be other speeches by TOAD during the evening.)

ADDRESS . . . BY TOAD

(MAIN POINTS—Our Prison System—the Canals of Old England—How to Horse-Deal—The Rights and Duties of Property-Owners)

SONG . . . BY TOAD.

(Composed by himself.)

OTHER COMPOSITIONS BY TOAD will be sung in the course of the evening by the . . . COMPOSER.

The idea pleased him greatly, and he worked very hard and got all the letters finished by noon. At that time, a small and rather shabby weasel came to the door, asking timidly whether he could do anything for the gentlemen. Toad swaggered out and found it was one of the prisoners of the previous evening, very respectful and anxious to please. He patted him on the head, shoved the bundle of invitations into his paw, and told him to deliver them as fast as he could, and if he came back again in the evening, there might be a dime for him. The poor weasel seemed quite grateful, and hurried off eagerly to do his mission.

The other animals came back to lunch, very cheerful after a morning on the river. Mole, who had been feeling a bit guilty about leaving Toad alone, expected to find him sulky or depressed. Instead, Toad was so pleased and puffed up that the other animals began to suspect something.

As soon as the meal was over, Toad thrust his paws deep into his trouser pockets and remarked casually, "Well, look after yourselves, you fellows! Ask for anything you want!" He went swaggering off in the direction of the garden, where he wanted to think out an idea or two for his coming speeches. Then the Rat caught him by the arm.

Toad suspected what was going on, and he did his best to get away. But when the

Badger took him firmly by the other arm he began to see that the game was up. The two animals conducted him into a small office, shut the door, and put him into a chair. Then they both stood in front of him, while Toad sat silent and glared at them ill-humoredly.

"Now, look here, Toad," said the Rat. "It's about this banquet. I'm very sorry to have to speak to you like this. But we want you to understand clearly, once and for all, that there are going to be no speeches and no songs. Try and understand that we're not arguing with you. We're just telling you."

Toad saw that he was trapped. They understood him, they saw through him, they had got ahead of him. His pleasant dream was shattered.

"Can't I sing them just one LITTLE song?" he pleaded.

"No, not ONE little song," replied the Rat firmly, though his heart bled as he noticed how poor disappointed Toad's lip was trembling. "It's no good, Toady. You know very well that your songs are all conceit and boasting and vanity, and that your speeches are all self-praise and gross exaggeration and—and—"

"And hot air," added Badger.

"It's for your own good, Toady," went on

the Rat. "You know you MUST turn over a new leaf sooner or later. Now seems a good time to begin. It's a sort of turning point in your career. Believe me, saying this hurts me as much as it hurts you."

Toad thought silently for a long time. At last he raised his head, and traces of strong emotion showed on his face. "You have won, my friends," he said brokenly. "It was only a small thing that I asked—merely to let myself flourish in the limelight for one last evening. Applause, you know, always seems to bring out my best qualities. However, you are right, I know, and I am wrong. From now on, I will be a very different Toad. You will never need to blush for me again. But, oh dear, this is a hard world!"

And, pressing his handkerchief to his eyes, he left the room, stumbling a little.

"Badger," said the Rat, "I feel like a brute."

"O, I know, I know," said the Badger gloomily. "But it had to be done. This good fellow has got to live here, and be respected. Would you want him to be a laughingstock, mocked and jeered at by stoats and weasels?"

"Of course not," said the Rat. "And, speaking of them, it's lucky we came upon that little weasel, just as he was starting out with Toad's invitations. I had a look at one or two, and they were simply ridiculous. I took them all, and right now Mole is writing out plain, simple invitation cards."

At last the time for the banquet drew near. Toad, who had gone to his bedroom, was still sitting there sadly. Resting his head on his paw, he thought long and deeply. Then his face began to clear, and he smiled. He started giggling shyly. At last he got up, locked the door, closed the curtains, collected all the chairs in the room and arranged them in a semicircle, and stood in front of them, swelling visibly. He bowed, coughed twice, and began to sing to his imaginary audience:

TOAD'S LAST LITTLE SONG!
The Toad—came—home!
There was panic in the parlors and terror in the halls,
There was crying in the cow-sheds and shrieking in the stalls,

When the Toad—came—home!
When the Toad—came—home!
There was smashing in of window and crashing in of door,
There was triumph over weasels that fainted on the floor,
When the Toad—came—home!
Bang! go the drums!

The trumpeters are tooting and the
soldiers are saluting,
And the cannon they are shooting and the
motorcars are hooting,
As the—Hero—comes!

Shout—Hoo-ray!
And let each one of the crowd try and
shout it very loud,
In honor of an animal of whom you're all
so proud,
For it's Toad's—great—day!

He sang this very loud, with great expression. When he was done, he sang it all over again.

Then he heaved a deep sigh—a long, long, long sigh.

Then he dipped his hairbrush in the water jug, parted his hair in the middle, and plastered it down very straight and sleek on each side of his face. Unlocking the door, he went quietly down the stairs to greet his guests, who he knew must be gathering in the drawing room.

All the animals cheered when he entered, and crowded around to congratulate him and say nice things about his courage and his cleverness. But Toad only smiled faintly, and murmured, "Not at all!" Otter came forward with a shout, threw his arm round Toad's neck, and tried to take him around the room in a sort of triumphal parade. But Toad pulled away, mildly saying, "Badger was the mastermind. The Mole and the Water Rat did most of the real fighting. I merely served in the ranks." The animals were most puzzled and surprised by this unexpected attitude. Toad himself felt, as he moved from one guest to the other, that his modest responses were making everyone most interested and curious.

The Badger had ordered the best of everything, and the banquet was a great success. There was much talking and laughter and joking among the animals, but through it all Toad just murmured pleasant nothings to the animals on either side of him. Occasionally he glanced at the Badger and the Rat, and he always found them staring at each other with their mouths open. This satisfied him enormously. Some of the younger animals started whispering to each other that Toad was not as amusing as he used to be in the good old days, and they began knocking on the table and crying "Toad! Speech! Speech from Toad! Sing, Mr. Toad!" But Toad only shook his head gently, raised one paw in mild protest, encouraged his guests to help themselves to more food, and asked about their families.

He was indeed a changed Toad!

After this memorable evening, the four animals continued to lead their lives (so rudely interrupted by civil war) in great joy and contentment. Toad sent a handsome necklace of gold and pearls to the jailer's daughter, along with a letter that even the Badger admitted was modest, grateful, and appreciative. Toad also properly thanked and repaid the engine driver for all his assistance. Under a great deal of pressure from the Badger, Toad even located the bargewoman and paid her back for her horse. (Toad kicked terribly at this, claiming that he was only a tool of Fate used to punish a horrid woman who couldn't tell a real gentleman when she saw one. The amount involved, however, was not very great, as it turned out that the Gypsy's evaluation of the horse was approximately correct.)

Sometimes, during long summer evenings, the Friends would take a stroll together in the Wild Wood, and it was pleasant to see how respectfully they were greeted by the residents there. The mother weasels would bring their young ones to the doors and say, pointing, "Look, baby! There goes the great Mr. Toad! And that's the gallant Water Rat, a terrible fighter, walking along with him! And yonder comes the famous Mr.

Mole, of whom you have often heard your father tell!" But when their children were naughty, they would quiet them by saying that if they didn't behave, the terrible gray Badger would come and get them. This was awfully unfair to Badger, who, although he cared little about Society, was rather fond of children. Still, it never failed to be effective.

Afterword

About the Author

The adventurous Water Rat; kind, sensible Mole; and foolish, boastful Toad were the creations of Kenneth Grahame, a Scottish banker. When you learn a bit about the author, you begin to wonder which was more real to him: the lighthearted, amusing world he invented, or the difficult, often sad world in which he lived.

Grahame was born in 1859, the third of what were eventually four children. His parents were a handsome, well-liked couple, but his father drank heavily. The family lived near the sea, and little Kenneth developed a passionate love of what Rat later called "messing about in boats." His early childhood seemed a happy and carefree one.

But fate was not kind to the Grahames for long. When Kenneth was five, a baby brother was born, and just a few days later Mrs. Grahame became ill with scarlet fever. (Scarlet fever is rarely dangerous today, but in the days before antibiotics, it was a feared killer.) She lived for only two weeks. On the day she died, little Kenneth began showing symptoms of the disease. Faced with the fact that his wife was dead, leaving him with a newborn baby and a sick little boy, Mr. Grahame fell apart. He turned his back on the children, got drunk, and stayed that way. Frantic servants contacted his mother, who arrived to care for the baby and poor sick Kenneth.

Once Kenneth was out of danger, it was decided that the children would go live with their mother's mother, "Granny Ingles," in the south of England. They never lived with their father again. He eventually moved to France and had little contact with them.

Granny Ingles was kind to the Grahame children, but they grew up rather wild and alone, with few playmates their own age. Kenneth was a bright student and would have liked to attend Oxford University, but his uncle John (who had supported the children since their father's abandonment) refused to send him. Instead, he told Kenneth, now 19, to take a job as a clerk at the Bank of England. He obediently did so, and by the time he was

38 he had been promoted to a senior position as Secretary of the Bank.

Kenneth was a responsible man, and he worked hard at his bank duties. But it was clear that his heart was never really in his work. What he loved to do was write happy, magical fantasies about childhood. His stories and essays appeared in popular magazines, and in 1895 he published a book titled *The Golden Age*, which featured the adventures of a family of five children. Three years later he followed with a similar book titled *Dream Days*. Both were popular, and Kenneth became a well-known writer. About that same time he married Elspeth Thomson, the step-daughter of a bank client, and the following year they had their only child, a boy they named Alistair.

The Wind in the Willows exists because of Alistair. The book is a lovely legacy of a child whose own life was odd and, eventually, tragic. Alistair was born blind in one eye. His mother and father seemed quite childlike in their own way (their letters to each other are written almost entirely in baby-talk), and they didn't seem to have any idea how to be parents, especially parents of a child with a disability. Elspeth insisted that the boy was brilliant and perfect in every way, and no one was allowed to criticize him. Kenneth was a little more realistic about "Mouse," as they called their son, but he too refused to discipline the boy. As a result, Alistair grew up badly spoiled and, apparently, quite unpleasant to be around. Elspeth's and Kenneth's letters are full of stories of Alistair slapping his playmates "because he wanted to," kicking his nanny, and verbally abusing his parents. It never seemed to occur to either parent to correct his behavior.

Kenneth was a very poor disciplinarian, but he was an excellent storyteller. When Alistair was only a toddler, Kenneth wrote to Elspeth, in his usual baby-language, that he'd been telling the boy a tale "in which a mole, a beever a badjer & a water-rat was characters & I got them terribly mixed up as I went along." The stories continued as Alistair grew up, and took shape as the adventures that we now know as *The Wind in the Willows.* As Alistair grew older, Toad became a more prominent character in the stories, and there seems to be a reason for that. One of Alistair's habits was to boast outrageously about his abilities and adventures—just like Toad, and Kenneth apparently modeled Toad after the boy. By gently making fun of Toad's foolishness, it seems that Kenneth was trying to warn

Alistair about the consequences of his actions.

In 1907, the Grahames were visited by a book agent named Constance Smedley, who encouraged Kenneth to follow up on the success of *The Golden Age* and *Dream Days* with another book of children's adventures. Kenneth resisted, saying that he was too busy at the bank, and that writing was such hard work for him that it was sheer torture. But he liked Miss Smedley and she stayed for dinner. When she overheard Alistair's bedtime story, and learned that Kenneth had been making up stories about Mole, Rat, and Toad for years, she saw the possibilities at once. The real work was already done, she pointed out; all Kenneth had to do now was to put the stories into book form. After giving it some thought, Kenneth realized she was right. He completed the book in just a few months.

The book was not an immediate success. British readers expected something like *The Golden Age*, and they didn't know what to make of talking animals or a toad that drove a motorcar. But after Kenneth sent a copy of the book to American President Theodore Roosevelt (who was a great fan of his earlier books), Roosevelt himself wrote a note to an American publisher, saying *The Wind in the Willows* was "such a beautiful thing that

Scribner *must* publish it." Scribner did, and the book did very well in the United States and, later, Britain.

Sadly, the success of *The Wind in the Willows* did not work any magic on the lives of the Grahame family. Sales of the book allowed Kenneth to retire from the bank, but he never published anything significant again. Elspeth grew more childishly eccentric as she aged. And Alistair, after withdrawing from two high schools because he could not get along with his fellow students, finally enrolled at Oxford University. The week before his twentieth birthday, he was struck by a train and killed. It was clear that he had committed suicide, but his parents—unrealistic to the end about their son—insisted that his death was accidental. Kenneth Grahame himself died in 1932.

The Wind in the Willows has been a children's and adult's favorite for almost a hundred years. Its offspring include several movie versions, a Broadway musical, puzzles, games, and even a sequel (written by an author other than Kenneth). But the greatest triumph of *The Wind in the Willows* may be the way that it, despite the sadness that clung to the family closest to its creation, has brought joy and laughter to millions.

About the Book

A famous poet once wrote, "How do I love thee? Let me count the ways." About *The Wind in the Willows*, readers who have made it a favorite since its publication in 1908 might well say, "How do we love *it*? Let us count the ways!" For when you ask fans of the book (let's call it *WITW*) why they enjoy it, their enthusiasm is really overwhelming.

If you want evidence, you might look up *WITW* on the online bookseller, Amazon.com, and read some of the reviews that readers have posted there. You'll find more than 80 such reviews. Here are a few comments from them:

"It's an extraordinarily beautiful book."

"One of my all-time favorites."

"The stories are hilarious."

"It's adventurous, poetic, and humorous."

"The book is soaked in the beauty and power of nature."

"A brilliant, uplifting, funny, moving tale."

It wouldn't be surprising to find glowing reviews about a recent best-seller. But it's pretty amazing to find so many people that feel so strongly about a book that's nearly a century old. And on its surface, *WITW* doesn't sound all that great. After all, it's an old book, written by a banker in Victorian-era England. It features talking animals—but not your typical lovable, cuddly kittens and puppies. Instead you've got a rich, reckless toad with a passion for automobiles, a kindly mole, and an adventurous water rat. Toads, moles, and rats, to put it kindly, are not usually literary heroes.

But somehow author Kenneth Grahame makes it all work, and work brilliantly. To get an idea how he did it, let's look at three adjectives that one of the Amazon.com reviewers used to describe *WITW*: "adventurous, poetic, and humorous."

In what way is *WITW* adventurous? Well, the dictionary says an "adventure" is "an undertaking involving danger and unknown risks" or "an exciting or remarkable experience." From its very first page, *WITW* is filled with adventure of both types. Shy, timid Mole is suddenly overcome with the desire to venture forth into the unknown world. The soft, warm air of springtime is what calls him—and surely any student who has ever sat in a stuffy classroom, staring out the window at the inviting spring sunshine, knows exactly how Mole felt! Soon Mole meets Rat, and with Rat comes the delightful adventures of learning to boat and swim and generally become part of the river community. After that, Mole experiences a less pleasant, but very exciting kind of adventure when he becomes lost in the terrifying Wild Wood. Then it's off to meet Toad and engage in the disastrous adventure of the canary-colored cart; and later Toad steals a car, ends up in prison, and escapes disguised as a washerwoman . . .

Oh, yes; there's plenty of adventure.

And why would a reader call *WITW* "poetic"? Clearly not because it's written as an actual poem. Rather, the reviewer means that Grahame's writing is *like* poetry. A poem, typically, does not tell a straightforward story. Instead, the poet uses language in ways that draw forth an emotional response from the reader. For example, when Mole is entering the Wild Wood, Grahame could have simply written, "It was a cold winter afternoon. Mole was feeling cheerful as he entered the Wild Wood. He didn't expect anything bad to happen."

Instead, Grahame writes this:

> **It was a cold still afternoon with a hard steely sky overhead, when he slipped out of the warm parlor into the open air. The country lay naked and leafless around him. He liked the bareness of the winter landscape, and with great cheerfulness he**

> **headed towards the Wild Wood, which lay before him low and threatening, like a black reef in some quiet southern sea.**
>
> **There was nothing to alarm Mole at first. Twigs crackled under his feet and logs tripped him, but that was all fun and exciting. It led him on, and he walked further to where the light was dimmer, and trees crouched nearer and nearer, and holes looked like ugly mouths on either side.**

The first version would have given you the same basic information as the way that Grahame wrote it. But what a difference there is between the two! The sky was "steely"; the Wild Wood lay "low and threatening, like a black reef." As the light grew "dimmer"the trees "crouched" like animals about to spring, and the holes resembled "ugly mouths." Grahame's poetic use of language makes it very clear to the reader (although poor Mole doesn't yet realize it) that this Wild Wood is a frightening, unfriendly place.

One of the most strikingly poetic parts of *WITW* is its most famous chapter: "The Piper at the Gates of Dawn." In it, Rat and Mole travel down the river at night in search of Portly, the missing baby otter. Drawn on by the sound of faint but haunting music, they are eventually led to the sleeping Portly, watched over by none other than the nature god, Pan. According to Greek mythology, Pan was half man and half goat. He wandered about playing beautiful music on his pan-pipes, which were constructed of river reeds. Kenneth Grahame's own great love of the power and mystery of nature comes through clearly in his beautiful description of Pan and the little animals' response to him:

> **[Mole] would not have dared to raise his eyes, but although the piping had stopped, the summons seemed more urgent than ever. He could not refuse, even if Death himself was waiting to strike him. Trembling, he raised his humble head. And there, in that utter clearness of the coming dawn, he looked in the very eyes of the Friend and Helper. He saw the backward sweep of the curved horns, gleaming in the growing daylight. He saw the stern, hooked nose between the kindly eyes that looked down on them humorously, while the bearded mouth broke into a half-smile. He saw the rippling muscles on the arm that lay across the broad chest, the long graceful hand still holding the pan-pipes. He saw the splendid curves of the shaggy limbs. Last of all, nestling between His very hooves, sleeping**

soundly, Mole saw the little, round, pudgy, childish form of the baby otter.

On nearly every page of *WITW*, you can find such examples of Grahame's joy in the use of language—a use that can, truly, be called poetic.

Finally, a reader called *WITW* "humorous." Well, who can argue with that? While the interaction of Rat and Mole has plenty of humorous moments, it is Mr. Toad of Toad Hall who provides most of *WITW's* comedy. Toad doesn't mean to be funny, but he is, almost constantly. Has there ever been a character who was more boastful, conceited, foolish and impulsive; so completely blind to the errors of his ways? And yet you have to like Toad; he's warm-hearted, generous, and great fun to be with. One of Toad's most amusing characteristics is his lightning-fast changes of opinion. For example, one minute he's crazy about his wonderful canary-colored horse-drawn cart. But then he is driven off the road by a speeding automobile. Instantly, his old love is forgotten:

And to think I never KNEW!" went on the Toad in a dreamy monotone. "All those wasted years that lie behind me, I never knew, never even DREAMED! But

> **NOW—now that I know, now that I fully realize! What dust-clouds shall spring up behind me as I speed on my reckless way! What carts I shall fling carelessly into the ditch in the wake of my magnificent progress! Horrid little carts—common carts—canary-colored carts!**

His patient friends, of course, are the ones who suffer from Toad's thoughtless changes of heart, and their efforts to rescue and reform him provide some of the *WITW*'s most amusing moments.

Adventure, poetry, and humor—these are some of the elements that have made *The Wind in the Willows* a beloved favorite for so many years. Now almost 100 years after its publication, new readers continue to discover its charms.

If you liked
The Wind in the Willows,
you might be interested in other
books in the Townsend Library.

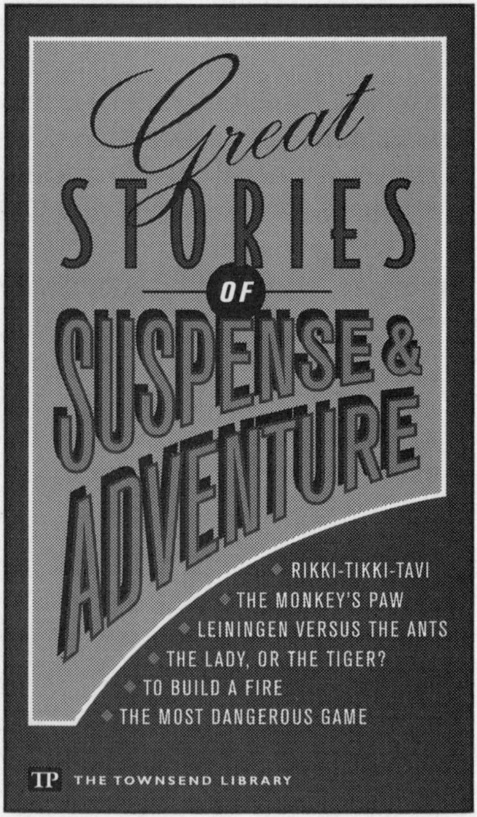

continued on the following pages

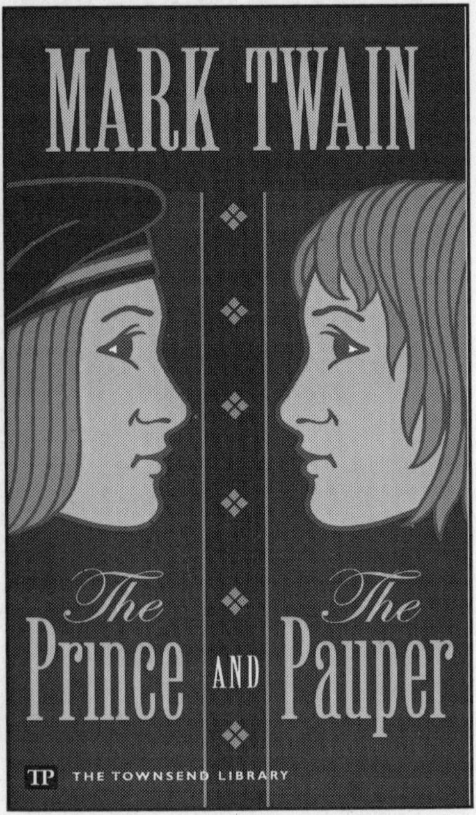
MARK TWAIN
The Prince and The Pauper
TP THE TOWNSEND LIBRARY

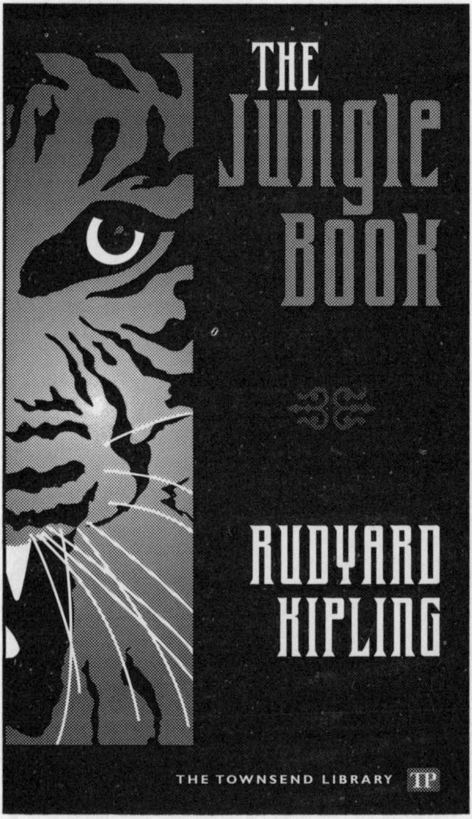
THE
Jungle
Book
RUDYARD
KIPLING
THE TOWNSEND LIBRARY

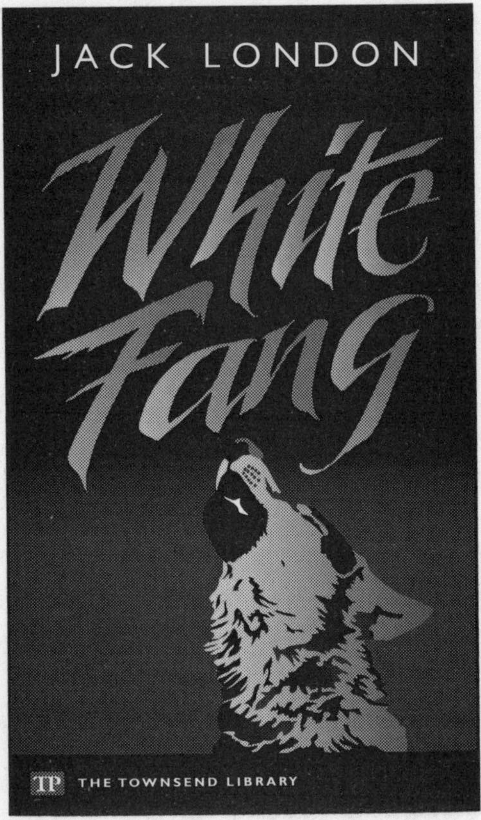
JACK LONDON
White Fang
TP THE TOWNSEND LIBRARY

Narrative of the Life of
FREDERICK
DOUGLASS
An
American
Slave
Written
by
Himself
TP THE TOWNSEND LIBRARY

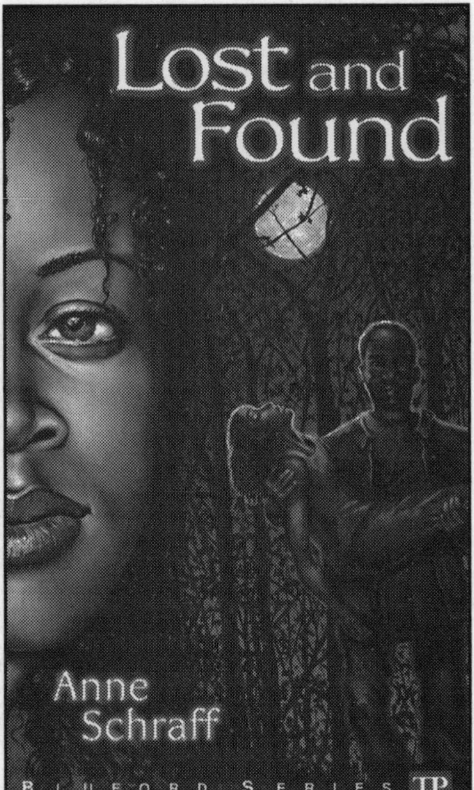
Lost and Found
Anne Schraff
BLUFORD SERIES
TP

The Bully
Paul Langan
TP BLUFORD SERIES

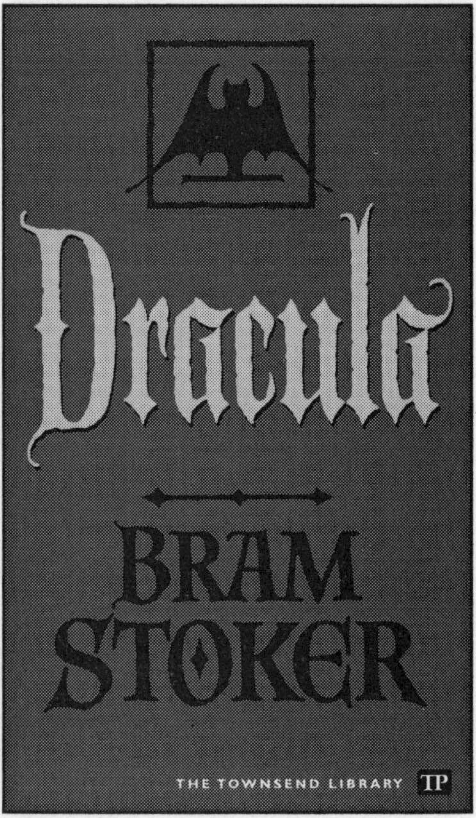
Dracula
BRAM
STOKER
THE TOWNSEND LIBRARY
TP

TARZAN
OF THE APES
EDGAR RICE BURROUGHS
TP THE TOWNSEND LIBRARY

CHARLOTTE BRONTË
JANE EYRE
TP THE TOWNSEND LIBRARY